Father Brown's Home for Boys

Father Brown's Home for Boys

WILLIAM J. O'SHEA

WILLIAM J. O'SHEA
WEST FRANKFORT

for Susan,

Contents

PROLOGUE

The 1960's were a turbulent time in our history. Our leaders were assassinated, America was bogged down in Vietnam, casualty numbers fought for space with Anti-War and Civil Rights movements on the front pages of every newspaper and for the lead story on the nightly news programs. Concurrently, while the world was distracted by these problems, the monsters who preyed on children thrived. Even if they were caught, there was practically no prosecution of these predators. Their crimes against innocent children were called "*Fondling*" or at worst "*Molestation*", those who were charged were given probation.

In the Catholic Church, across the globe, pedophile priests also thrived. They operated with impunity. If they were caught, their evil deeds were covered up by a Church that was afraid of public scrutiny and the predators would be transferred to another parish, where nobody knew of their crimes and there was also a new flock of children for them to prey upon.

Even when a priest behaved so outrageously that it became common knowledge that he was a child predator the police were never involved, rather he would be sent to a retreat in the South West where he would be *treated* and released back into the world like a vampire risen. These monsters weren't hiding under the bed, they were bold in their behaviors, and since everything was covered up they were above the law.

This predatory behavior by clergy didn't start in the 1960's, but it reached new heights then with all the other evils that plagued the world. Like other evil men throughout history these predator priests must have thought that God was on their side. He was not. In fact God had champions who conquered evil every day. These men would be held accountable for their sins, regardless of who they were.

Chapter 1: Area 3 Homicide

"Where's that Diaper Dick?" the voice came from an office down at the end of the hall on the third floor of the Area Three Detective's building.

"I'm right here." I said as I entered the room.

"Oh, um we need you to chaperone this kid for a homicide interview." Homicide dicks never apologized. They were at the top of the heap. These two were new to me. Actually I was new to Youth, and technically, the Detective Division. I was at the bottom of the heap.

The one with the big mouth told me his name when I pointed at my notebook with a pencil. Jake Flannigan was dressed like his partner, Stanley Dombrowski, tailor made silk suits, hand-made Italian shoes, with enough diamonds and gold jewelry to buy a new Caddy, which I'm sure they both already drove.

"The kid says his mother cleans houses in Hyde Park, doesn't know where she is. We can't find any other relatives so you're it." The boy, nervous but not scared, was about 14. Flannigan filled me in on what was happening and that's when I knew why the boy wasn't scared. They had already interviewed him, gotten the whole story and were just playing by the rules for some reason and putting me in the middle.

The boy lived with his mother in the ghetto, not in the

Projects but close enough that it didn't matter. They had the second floor of a frame two flat on 42nd and Giles Avenue. His mother probably worked very hard to afford an apartment, such as it was. The murder victim lived on the first floor. Her name was Sheila Harper, she was in her early twenties and had been stabbed about once for every year she had lived.

One of her *boyfriends*, one of many apparently, was seen at her house shortly before the supposed time of the murder. He drove a sky blue Buick Electra 225 convertible and had parked it in front of the house where it had been seen by a number of people.

They went through the questions with the boy whose name was Franklin Palmer. He parroted the answers they had already gone over with him before I arrived.

"Did you hear screaming?" Flannigan asked.

"Yes"

"Where was it coming from?"

"Downstairs"

"What happened then?"

"I heard a door slam."

"And.......what did you do then Franklin."

The kid wasn't remembering his lines quickly enough for Flannigan. Dombrowski was apparently the senior member of the pair. The only thing he had said so far was his name, and I'd bet he had to practice that all the time.

"Uh....I went and looked out the window, and I saw Johnny Slater run out and jump in his car and drive away. He was wearing a blue suit that was the same color as his car. I know it was Johnny cause I see him come by She-she's house all the time, almost every day."

He had skipped over the questions that they were going to ask and the rest of the story poured out of the boy. I could tell Flannigan wanted to strangle the kid.

"Well, okay...Officer...?" Flannigan had never bothered to ask my name and I had not volunteered.

"Kelly, Jim Kelly." I answered and asked, "Is what *okay* Detective?"

Even though I was paid the same as a rookie detective, I was in the Youth Division and called a *Youth Officer*.

"What? What?" Steam was starting to come out of the starched collar of the detective's shirt. "What do you mean, '*What*'? You heard him, right? We didn't coerce the kid, right?"

There were a lot of stories of police *coercion* in the newspapers. The last thing these homicide dicks needed was to be caught putting words in this kid's mouth that could put a guy in the electric chair.

"Do you mind if I have a little time to talk with Franklin? Alone?" I asked.

Dombrowski found his voice. "What do you want to talk to him about? You heard what he said. The guy did it and ran out of the house. That's it! Just say that you witnessed the interview and it went according to Hoyle." I didn't say anything. This wasn't a card game.

After an uncomfortable period of time, Flannigan said that they had to finish booking Slater and read him his rights. They left us alone.

"So Franklin, where do you go to school?"

"Parkman." He was still in elementary school. He was a little big for grammar school.

"Why aren't you in high school?"

"I'm in Special Ed." He was dancing around now that he hadn't been fed the answers. I let it go, I had another place to go.

"How long have you known She-She?" I used the name he had used to refer to his neighbor Shelia.

"I know her for a while."

"This guy Johnny, he comes by there every day?"

"Yes."

"And how long does he stay."

"I don't know."

"Oh, but you knew he was there today right? How long was he there today?" I asked.

"Long enough," he said. There was a little something more in his voice.

"Did She-She have any other men come by her house?"

"Yes," more *something* in his voice.

"How come you call her "She-She"? Isn't her name Sheila?"

"She said I could call her She-She." There was a little defiance in his voice now, because she had allowed him to call her by a pet name.

"She was a hooker, huh Franklin?"

"No," came the quick response.

"Come on, what do you think all those men were doing Franklin?" Now my voice had something in it.

"I don't know," he lied.

"You couldn't stand it that all those men could be with her and...." My voice was sympathetic, I let the last part go unsaid.

He started to cry. I spoke to him calmly and quietly, and let him tell me all about it. Johnny was her pimp and he went there to collect every day. Franklin blamed Johnny for what She-She was. He loved her in his newly developing puberty way.

Sheila had kick started the boy's sex life, allowing him to *visit* when she had nothing else to play with. After Johnny left, Franklin had gone downstairs, thinking that he could be man enough to tell her that she didn't need Johnny or the other men any longer because he was going to be her man now.

When he tried to kiss her and make love to her like a man, she had slapped him and told him to get back upstairs. She had turned him on. He turned her off. There was a thin line between love and hate.

Flannigan and Dombrowski were coming down the hall when I walked out of the interview room with Franklin in handcuffs. The look on their faces spoke before they did.

"What are you doing? Where do you think you're going with him?" Dombrowski was getting more talkative. I wondered how he was going to take it.

"He did it." That was all I said. The look on Franklin's face and the kid's tear streaked cheeks backed me up.

"What do you mean, 'He *did it*'"? Dombrowski was asking a lot of questions that I didn't need to answer, but I couldn't resist.

"He did it. He killed Sheila Harper with a knife in her bedroom. Clear enough?"

"That's what the pimp said," Flannigan said to Dombrowski, as though no one else was present.

"Shut up!" Dombrowski was definitely the senior man, because Flannigan shut up.

Dombrowski screamed at me. "You're not getting this pinch! You put a story in that kid's mouth. You say you have a confession. Did you read him his rights before you took that confession?"

Dombrowski was getting all senior detective on me. Reading people their rights was all the rage right now. Everybody was reading people their rights, although no one was getting their rights.

"Kids don't have rights you dumb polock." I said, as I walked the kid down the stairs one flight to the Youth Office. Dombrowski would have shot me, if there hadn't been so many witnesses.

Chapter 2: Piggly Wiggly

"Three for a dollar?" what am I going to do with three cans of beans? Mrs. Curtin asked with her usual Irish temper and loud enough for anyone in the next aisle to hear.

"You eat them, Ma," Her dutiful son answered. Clearly getting tired of answering questions that had no answer, but Curtin took care of his mother regardless of how she acted. Born on New Year's Day in the year 1900, Mrs. Curtin was in her late sixty's now and not mellowing in her old age.

"Don't sass me, Tom. You know what I mean. How much for one? That's what I want to know. Thirty-three cents, thirty-four, what?" She wasn't giving in on this one.

Curtin put three cans in the cart and acknowledged that the store was trying to cheat her and that it was his fault. She probably had enough money to buy the store but that wasn't the issue, a penny was a penny. That's how the old country Irish were raised on the south side of Chicago at the turn of the century.

Her dear departed husband, Paddy, had come from Ireland on a Friday, in 1920, to escape British custody. An Irish Alderman made him a Chicago Police Officer and stationed him on the corner of 47th and Ashland Avenue, the following Monday morning. He had such a thick brogue that even the Irish citizens of the Back of the Yards neighborhood couldn't understand him.

They had met in a sort of prearranged Irish proper way. They married and had six children, also the Irish way. The typical Irish American family, a politician, a contractor, a fireman, a policeman, and of course, a priest. The one girl, Elizabeth, who was doted on, married into the Sicilian Mafia, which created a family crisis, but she was a tough Irish lass like her mother and told everybody where they could go if they didn't like it. The priest was the first to welcome her new husband to the family. The rest were basically afraid of her and relented.

Padraig Curtin didn't live much past his retirement in 1956. Curtin ended up being the last one to leave the nest which meant he could never leave the nest. He'd been close to marriage a couple of times, all the prospects were given *"the treatment"* by Mrs. Curtin. They ran as fast as their legs could carry them. Yet, Curtin loved his mother in an Irish kind of way and took care of her as he was expected to do by tradition.

"That's enough. I'm tired. Let's go home," she said. Curtin was delighted and turned back toward the front of the store, his mother didn't. She kept pushing her cart to the end of the aisle.

"Fuck out of my way old bitch!" Curtin turned to see a man shove his mother's cart out of his way and proceed to the next aisle without so much as a glance in his direction. He was a big guy compared to Curtin's 5'8". He was probably over six foot and 40 pounds heavier. That was all he saw as Curtin ran to catch his mother who had stumbled backwards. She would have fallen if he hadn't caught her.

Mrs. Curtin was so stunned she was speechless. Finally she regained her wits and said, "Did you see what he did?"

"Ma, are you all right?" Curtin was clearly more concerned about his mother than worrying about the offender.

"Oh, I'm okay. Let's go," she said.

"I'll bet if Paddy was here, he would have given that ruffian a sound thrashing," she said, as she pushed her cart toward the front of the store, implying that Curtin wasn't the man his father was, which was accurate, he wasn't.

When Curtin paid for the groceries, always with cash, he purposely left a few coins on the counter and after he had his mother and the groceries settled in the car he told her that he had left his change on the counter and he had to go back to get it.

Mrs. Curtin totally understood that money was not to be left on a counter and was scolding him about forgetting as he closed her door and started back into the store. It wasn't about the change but he always felt uneasy lying to his mother.

Curtin found the offender in the liquor aisle. Where else? The guy was bending over examining two bottles of cheap vodka. Curtin didn't care what he was doing. He picked up a gallon jug of cheap wine by the neck and started down the aisle toward the man who had assaulted his mother. He was the cop in the family. It was time for some street justice.

When he was a few steps from the guy he picked up speed and started to swing the jug like he was bowling. He bowled his best strike, smashing the guy in the head with all the force he could muster. The heavy bottle exploded and so did the guy's head. Curtin didn't give it a second's thought.

He calmly walked out of the store, got into his car, and drove out of the lot.

"Did you get it?" Mrs. Curtin asked, then added, "what is that smell?"

"No, Ma, I didn't get it. Somebody else got it. They were mopping the floor, I must have stepped in something." He answered, realizing that he had Pisano and probably blood all over him. Mrs. Curtin scolded him all the way home. He deserved it for not taking proper care of his mother.

Curtin looked into it the next day. The ambulance personnel had saved the guy, believe it or not, and everybody at the Piggly Wiggly developed a case of amnesia regarding any questions from the police, who also weren't very interested because the victim was a known sleaze bag. That caused interest to fade away, and after a few weeks Curtin and his mother were back shopping.

Chapter 3: 42nd & Indiana Avenue

Poc had nowhere to go, but he couldn't stop moving. He was in a strange place where all the people were black. There were cars and people going everywhere just like in Saigon, but this wasn't Saigon. He just kept walking and watching for anyone with the robes on.

Some people spoke to him although he couldn't understand them. He spoke some English, more than the other boys, but he couldn't understand these black people. Someone grabbed his arm and he pulled away. He ran down an alley coming out on an even busier street.

Then Poc ran into a policeman, right into him. The policeman was big and black and he had two silver guns. He held onto Poc until he stopped struggling, but kept a hold on him sensing that the boy would try to break away, which he did several times. He didn't want the police. They were just as bad. He wanted....he didn't know what he wanted. The big policeman wasn't hurting him. When he realized this, he also realized that the man was talking to him slowly, so he could understand.

"Where'd you come from, boy?" the man said.

Poc understood, but wasn't answering. He just kept a blank look on his face and waited for a chance to get away. That was what he had been doing since he left Vietnam, looking for a chance to get away.

Chapter 4: Area 3 Lobby

It was late when I finished all the paperwork on Franklin Palmer and got ready to take him over to the Audy Home. Chicago had the largest juvenile prison in the world, even though they called it a home. At the turn of the century the old orphanage/jail had burned down and for years children were housed with adult prisoners, which was a daily nightmare for all. Finally, they passed legislation that ended that practice and the women at Hull House and the Chicago Bar Association established housing for children who were wards of the State and they also established the first juvenile court.

There were three categories: delinquent, abused and neglected. In recent years these children were separated and more importantly, treated separately. Sounds like a no brainer. Anyway the place is named after Arthur J. Audy, who served in WWII and was a live-in superintendent for a few years when he died of a heart attack at age 34. His widow convinced the city to name the place after him as a memorial tribute. The official name has changed several names but it is still referred to as the Audy Home.

Franklin and I were the last ones to leave the office, I left the lights on. We walked down the creaky wooden stairs, with the hand worn railings, to the lobby of the station house and started for the door when one of the desk men called out to me.

"Hey, Kelly, you got another one. Don't forget that gook." He pointed over to the bench running along the wall where a little Asian boy was handcuffed to the radiator. At least it was summer. He was small and thin as a rail, thick black hair and big dark eyes, maybe 10 or 12 years old.

Joe Flynn knew I didn't like the word "*Gook*". We had both gone to Vietnam in the early days of the war, only we came back different. For one thing, I came back a lot sooner than Flynn. He did his entire tour while I received a medical discharge, so he didn't consider me a real veteran. I didn't care because I didn't consider myself a veteran either, although I had received a Purple Heart, and Flynn didn't.

He was shot, although he wasn't injured badly enough to get a medical discharge. Flynn didn't get his Purple Heart because his paperwork was never filed. He was a jerk in the army too, I suspected. Now all he did was complain about his leg. Nobody cared, but it did get him a job on the desk.

The reason I didn't consider myself a veteran was because I was the cook. Army personnel carried M16's while my weapon was a spoon. I didn't deserve a medal, I was blown up by a field cook stove. But the other five guys in the tent were killed, so they had to send their parents something to go with the little box of ashes, and I got a Purple Heart too.

I had only been in Phou Bai for a month or so, we were playing cards one night after about six days of monsoon rain. Everything in our cook tent was soaked and the sergeant got the idea to use a couple of the field stove burners to dry out the tent.

They ran on gasoline which was the only abundant fuel in the field. Pressurized gasoline, from a five gallon tank, vaporized when it was passed through a tube over the burners and got hotter or cooler depending on how the flame was adjusted. I knew the mess sergeant had them turned up too high. I also knew better than to question him. I just kept an eye on my cards, and the field stove burners.

The first thing we heard was a loud ping, the others looked around. I started for the door. The explosion threw me out of the tent, they said thirty feet. I caught a piece of metal in my back which ended up being my ticket home.

I was in the next class for the Chicago Police Department. I didn't need two kidneys to be a cop.

"What are you talking about, Flynn?" I was tired and looking forward to going home. If I got another case now, I could be up all night.

Flynn nudged the desk sergeant and pointed at the kid. He looked up from his reports and saw me standing there. Sergeant Kern was a nice old German, but was the commandant of that desk. "That kid is lost or something Kelly and since you guys have no midnight crew, he's your responsibility."

"What do you mean he's lost or some..." I was interrupted as one of the double doors to the street crashed open and a little man stumbled into the lobby holding his chest. He made it to the desk and said something in Spanish to Sgt. Kern. He was dressed in a traditional Mexican shirt with black trousers and shoes. It was Friday night and he looked like he was dressed up.

Kern didn't understand a word and shook his head to illustrate the fact. "Speaky English?" Kern asked in what he thought was a Spanish accent.

The little guy took his hand away from his shirt and I saw that it was covered with blood. His shirt had a hole in the front with black powder burns around it. Someone had been pretty close when they had shot this man.

"Get me a wagon over here Flynn!" Kern shouted. Police paddy wagons were easier to get than ambulances at midnight on a Friday. Flynn was already on the phone to the dispatcher down at 11th and State.

Meanwhile the Mexican was talking a blue streak but nobody could understand a word. Kern kept asking him if he could speak English and who shot him. The guy didn't understand.

Then Flynn had an idea, for the first time in his life. There was a detective in Burglary who went to Mexico every year for his furlough. He always carried a stack of photos and would bend anyone's ear he could find to talk about his Mexican adventures. Everyone avoided him for that reason, especially right after he returned from furlough and would walk into the station and say "*Buenos Dias Senor Policias!!*"

"Cochran can speak Spanish," Flynn muttered.

The Mexican sank to the floor, nobody was doing anything to help him, including me. I had my prisoner next to me and on the other side was the little Asian boy, cuffed to the radiator. Franklin just looked at the guy. He had seen things like this before. The little Asian boy however had a look of wide eyed terror.

"I know!" Kern said, as if it was his idea all the time. "Call upstairs and tell Bobby Cochran to get down here!" Flynn already had the phone in his hand.

One of the other desk personnel came around and put a folded up fire rescue blanket under the guy's head. It was clear that the little man was fading. When Cochran came running down the stairs Kern yelled at him to talk some Spanish to the guy and find out who had shot him.

Cochran was hesitant and Kern yelled at him again. Cochran bent down to the dying man and when the man was finally able to fix his vision on Cochran, he said, "Who shooted you, Senor?"

The last thing the little man heard on this earth was everyone laughing, at Cochran. I unhooked the kid from the radiator, grabbed the paper Flynn waved at me and the three of us beat a hasty retreat from the station.

Chapter 5: Mario Petrocelli's kitchen

"You've been a bad boy, Mario, and now you have to be punished. You understand that, don't you?" No answer.

"And what a list. You poured gasoline on a hooker and set her on fire." No answer. It wasn't a question really.

"Your pregnant girlfriend was found floating in the lake with a bullet hole in her forehead. And I know the slug you put in her stomach was first so you could watch her face when you did it. You're really a sick puppy, you know that, Mario?" That got a grunt.

"Oh yes, your list is long, buddy, and impressive. You've killed a lot more people than I have, I think, because you like it so much. I, on the other hand always get paid one way or another. Although I do have to abide by my employer's specific wishes, such as in your case." No response from Mario.

"But funny thing is your own people signed off on you." That made his eyebrows go up. "It seems that you can be the most merciless, psychopathic killer in mob history and that is a badge of honor with you people, but screwing your partner's girlfriend is a capital offense. His wife he wouldn't mind, but the girlfriend, that's a different thing all together." Mario's eyes showed he now knew that there was nowhere to go but where he was going.

He was tied to a chair in his kitchen. He lived alone, since wife number three took the kid and left some time ago. The kitchen broom was tied to the back of the chair and his head was secured to the broomstick with cotton pads and surgical tape. It was all designed to leave no marks on the body.

"Well, now it's time to earn my ten grand." Mario just looked back with all the hatred he could convey with just his eyes. It was considerable. Curtin wouldn't have liked tangling with this guy on an even basis and was glad they had delivered him home practically unconscious from a long night out partying with his buddies. One of whom was the guy who had put out the contract for the present activity. It had been a birthday party, for Mario. Nice friends. They kill you on your birthday.

Curtin began to slowly peel away the surgical tape from the side of Mario's mouth, just a little bit. Then he took a hypodermic syringe out of his work bag and stuck the tip of the long needle into Mario's mouth. He was struggling now, the chair bouncing, but Curtin had his foot on the rung and his knee in Mario's crotch. He held his head steady with the other gloved hand.

"You should be happy. Your old buddy wanted it to look like a coronary, you know, natural death. He could have ordered something similar to what you do to people for fun and the Feds would still have paid for it."

Mario stopped struggling for a second and looked up. Curtin smiled at him. "That's right, your partner put the hit out on you and the Feds are paying for it. Happy Birthday."

Curtin pushed the needle in under Mario's tongue, where

the puncture mark would never be noticed, and injected the full vial of Digitalis into the struggling man. He didn't struggle long. Curtin got off him and started to take the bindings off of Mario's arms and legs.

Mario wasn't dead yet, but he was unconscious. His heart was strong, but the beats grew farther and farther apart. A lot of cops had second jobs. Some moved furniture or sold used cars, some worked as security guards. Curtin eliminated habitual criminals for the F.B.I.

Curtin finished cleaning up all of his stuff and as a little added flair of his own, he poured milk into a big bowl of Wheaties and put Mario face down in the bowl. Poor guy sitting in his own kitchen eating the breakfast of Champions and he pops a heart attack. He left quietly and hurried to his car. His mother had a doctor's appointment and he didn't want to hear it if he was late picking her up.

Chapter 6: Audy Home

I know how to take care of kids, not how to care *for* them. I took care so they didn't get away. Kids are quick, squirmy and always looking for a way to slip the knot. The little Asian boy, who had been cuffed to the radiator, tried to squirm out of my grasp three times before I got him secured in the back seat of the car. I tried to talk to him but he never made a sound, not even a grunt when I manhandled him into the back and cuffed him to the door handle. He couldn't have weighed more than 60 pounds.

I had a plain clothes car that had the back inside door handles disconnected to keep kids from opening the doors and jumping out when the car was moving. That had happened so often the handles were now disconnected at the factory.

Franklin Palmer just stood there the whole time I was wrestling with the little boy. He was either pretty slow or had believed his mother when she said *"that whore got what she deserved"* and that she would have him out by morning. I doubted it.

The little boy looked to be Vietnamese, certainly from Southeast Asia somewhere. I knew a few words of Vietnamese but when I tried them out there was no recognition from him, nor did he attempt to communicate in any way. He just stared out the window all the way to the Audy Home, like a weird tourist looking at sights never seen before.

An imposing structure, the Audy Home was big enough to house 500 kids. They averaged 750. It was over crowded despite the fact that it was so scary looking that you would think kids would do anything to keep from going there. In my job just the threat of sending someone to the Audy Home solved some delinquency problems in youthful offenders.

After pressing the button on the intercom, a voice asked my business and buzzed the door open after only a few words. There was a small hallway and another locked door at the top of a short staircase, it had a wired glass window in it but there was no one looking out. When we got to the top of the stairs, it buzzed open like magic and we walked passed a disinterested guard sitting behind a battered desk who should have checked my ID and had me sign in. If he didn't care, I didn't either.

I got Franklin booked into the detention side of the building all the while maintaining a firm grip on the Asian boy. When I took him to be checked in at the abused and neglected side I didn't know what nationality he was. I started filling out his incarceration form, they called it something else but that's what it was. I checked the boxes but kept the focus on him being the victim of something instead of just a lost child. If he was lost why hadn't someone called the police and reported it.

I didn't want to call him a runaway, which would categorize him as delinquent. I didn't want that. Most of the boxes were checked *unknown*. There were too many unknowns on this boy and I got curious. I knew better, the cat and curiosity cliché isn't undeserved.

I could have left him there and gone home to a well-deserved night of sleep but I let the cliché get the better of me and I hung around while they processed him. After a while a young woman in a nurse's uniform came out of an examining room and asked if I was the person who brought the boy in.

She was tall and slender, not skinny, more athletic. She had soft brown hair and eyes to match. She wore a nurse's cap I thought I had seen before and I noticed she had a Caduceus pin like the ones nurses wore in the army hospitals.

"Officer...?" she said, waiting for me to identify myself. Army nurses were officers and she sounded like she was used to being obeyed.

"Kelly," I said, trying to be nice about it. She was cute. She wasn't nice though.

"Kelly," she said it like a curse word. I just waited for the slap.

"Did you examine this boy? Do you know where he's been? Do you have anyone in custody?" Her voice got louder with every question.

"No, no, and finally no." I wasn't in the mood for twenty questions. Custody? What was she talking about? The kid was the one who was in custody.

"Come with me." She crooked her finger at me. I sort of didn't want to go but I could see there was no arguing with that finger, so I followed her.

The little boy was sitting on the table, there was an orderly sitting in the corner, looking bored. The boy was wearing a hospital gown, his clothes on the table next to him. They looked like rags really, more than clothes, worn shoes and patches on everything. She ignored them and moved to the boy. When she reached for the hospital gown he flinched away but she said something in Vietnamese and he relented. Then she pulled the smock from his shoulders. There were a million bruises on his little body.

Well, not a million, but hundreds easily. I could tell that they were not from the same beating, which is all it could have been, a beating. Many were purple, recently done. Some were older, yellow and fading. They were little round dots about a half inch apart.

I couldn't for the life of me think of what was used to do so much damage to this boy. Looking closely, I could see that the little round dots were everywhere on the boy. Someone had raged over this child, beating him mercilessly and repeatedly.

"Well?" The nurse was blaming me as the closest person with any responsibility. I didn't argue.

"Well what? I was just asked to bring him over here. I never saw him before about an hour ago." That lame excuse wasn't flying anywhere near satisfying the nurse. I remembered the case report that Flynn handed me and took the crumpled sheet from my jacket pocket. At the top someone had written in pencil, *Unknown Lost or Missing Person.*

When I looked at it more closely, I began to loosen my tie subconsciously, not wanting to tell her that there was nothing on the sheet to answer any of her questions. He was picked up by a beat officer, Cecil Washington, on 42nd and Indiana, a little earlier that day. A note at the bottom read, "Does not talk or understand English." That was all and it wasn't much.

"I'm sorry nurse...?" turn about being fair play.

"Miller, Kay Miller," she said it with pride and a little threateningly.

I cleared my throat, "Well, Kay...may I call you Kay?"

No answer was necessary. "Well, Nurse Miller, I don't know anything other than the boy was picked up on the south side earlier today..."

"South side!" she interrupted. "Does he look like he's from the south side to you?"

"South Vietnam, maybe." I said, trying to defuse the situation. "I noticed your pin. What rank were you when you were *In Country?*" I figured if I used a little army talk it might loosen her up a bit. I knew that nurses were all officers to protect them from the lower ranks. If I had to guess, she'd been a captain.

"How long were you there?" She asked, completely shooting down my balloon.

"Not very long, I got blown up," I answered sheepishly and truthfully. She glared at me.

"What are you going to do about this boy?" Back to reality.

"I'm going to find out what happened and take the proper action." How's that for an answer?

"Just what I expected." She was getting ready for another salvo.

"Wait!" I held up my hands protectively. "I'm going to do something. Give me a chance. Will you? I didn't know the boy was hurt. I couldn't get a word out of him. My Vietnamese is not as good as yours."

"His name is Poc and he speaks English as well." For the first time I realized that he had been following our conversation all along.

"What else did he tell you?" My turn now. I could tell by the look on her face that was the right question.

"He won't tell me anything." There was frustration in her voice. It was after midnight now, probably past both of our relief hours.

"I'll tell you what. You get him settled in and I'll hit the street first thing in the morning and try to find out what I can. That's the best I can do now, considering we're both in the same boat." Now we're buddies, right?

"We're not in any boat, Detective." The buddy thing was off. "I'm doing my job, you're not doing yours. What similarity do you see there?"

"Officer." I said, admitting the title.

"Officer?" She asked.

"I'm a Youth Officer. Although technically the same rank as a detective, they refer to us as *Officers*, not detectives." I could see that I went down a little in her estimation, if that was even possible.

"Whatever. Fine. You just get the hell out of here and I'll care for this boy." That was a dismissal like I'd never heard before.

"I'll be back tomorrow with some information," I guaranteed. She just looked me out the door, and I went. The orderly gave me a sympathetic look on the way out, but he wasn't about to draw attention to himself by defending me, no way.

Chapter 7: The Home

"Where the hell are they? Goddammit!! Answer me! You idiot. How did they get away?"

When there was the slightest pause the receiver of the rant said nervously, "We don't know how they got out. We have a call into the police liaison person and I am going to start contacting the local churches and social organizations, there's quite a number of..."

"You fucking idiot! Stupid son of a bitch! Don't be calling around telling everyone how stupid you are!"

"I haven't spoken to anyone yet."

"Then hit the streets, and take those other assholes with you. And if you don't come back with them you can all start packing. I think a trip back into the field would do you all good. Sharpen your attention skills." He thought it would be good example to the rest if a few of them were killed.

Chapter 8: The Curtin's

Curtin was surprised and happy to see his brother, Michael, sitting at the table with his mother when he arrived late. "Hi, Tommy," the carbon copy of Curtin's father said, showing that big Irish smile.

Curtin hated being called Tommy, but Michael was his older brother. He had certain privileges. Being a priest got him more privileges.

"Hi, Mick," Curtin answered. "I thought you were in Italy."

"Just got back." He was wearing a sport jacket with a white shirt and tie, nothing that looked remotely priestly. "Tommy, I wonder if you would mind if I took Ma to her doctor's appointment?"

Curtin wanted to kiss him. They played this little game for Ma, acting like it was so wonderful to take her to the doctor that they had to fight over the opportunity. "Okay, sure. You're not too tired? Jet lag or anything?" Curtin played it up.

"Enough, let's go." Mrs. Curtin said, getting up with her purse already in hand. "We're going to be late. You know how I hate to be late." Michael had wanted to leave 20 minutes ago, but she had delayed so she could be late. It would be Curtin's fault. She liked to have a little Irish spice in her life and Curtin was glad to provide it.

Smiling at each other. They said in unison, "yes, Ma".

Even though he had hardly slept, now that he had the rest of the day, he called into the office to see what was going on and what he could get into. He was really a workaholic. Besides doing these little side jobs for the Feds, the Chicago Police Intelligence Division was busy with Civil Rights, which no one was getting any of, Hippies against the war, or whatever was pissing them off on any given day. You name it, there was someone against it and the CPD needed to know who they were and what they were planning.

The lieutenant sent him out on a triple homicide, the killing of three Blackstone Rangers on the south side. The Rangers were the first organized black street gang in Chicago. Led by a man named Jeff Ford, his second in command was a man they called Black Jesus, they had been terrorizing the south side for years. In fact, Ford was already doing several life sentences for murder and associated crimes.

Curtin liked working in Intelligence, he could make his own hours as long as he produced, which was never a problem for him. He wished they had some black officers in the unit though, it would make a lot of this black militant stuff easier to infiltrate. But the lieutenant knew that Curtin had certain connections, which is why he got the job in the first place. He figured it was time to head down Indiana Avenue to get a shoe shine.

Chapter 9: Area 3 Youth Office

Arriving just on time, and hurrying up the stairs, I ran into Detective Dombrowski, literally. He brushed invisible filth off his tailored suit and grinned at me. "Lost your murderer, eh Kelly?" I didn't know what he was talking about and hurried past him up the stairs. Fuck him.

That curse turned around on me fast, Sergeant Toolis was waiting for me at the door and ushered me into his office with the rest of the people in the squad room looking at me as though he had an axe in his hand. I was the Thanksgiving turkey.

"What did you do last night?" Such a broad question was purposely designed to have no good answer.

"How about narrowing it down for me a little." I wasn't in the mood for guessing. That nurse and the kid were still on my mind.

"That kid that you took to the Audy Home, he got away and I'm getting calls from 11th Street." That was where Police Headquarters was located, 1101 South State Street. That great street. It was right across the street from the Crusaders Mission where derelicts lay around unconscious, soaked in their own urine.

The first thing I thought about was the Vietnamese boy and Nurse Miller. "I signed him in and left. If he got away, it's their fault." I defended myself.

"They said the boy walked out with you," he countered.

"How could he? He was naked, sitting on a table with the nurse and the orderly right there!" This was getting unbelievable.

"They didn't say anything about him being naked when he followed you out of the building. I think someone would have noticed that. Kelly, this is a murder suspect. We can't just blow it off and say you didn't see him walking out with you. What the hell did you do with him anyway?"

"Murder suspect? You mean Franklin Palmer?" Now I knew why Dombrowski was taunting me. I was relieved it wasn't Poc, even though a murderer, not a suspect in my estimation, had escaped.

"Who did you think we were talking about here? Come on, Kelly, get with it." Calls from downtown unhinged a lot of people out in the field.

"The Vietnamese boy." I answered, not really listening to the sergeant any longer. How could Franklin get out? I remembered leaving in a huff when I was dismissed by Nurse Miller, I didn't look to see if anyone was behind me. This wasn't my fault, but I could see how the people at the Audy Home weren't going to say that they screwed up. It just wasn't what passed for human nature in Chicago politics.

"Vietnamese boy!" Toolis was at the top of his voice, which wasn't that high considering he smoked three packs of unfiltered cigarettes a day.

"Yea, they had a little Vietnamese boy downstairs who was

lost or something and they dumped him on me when I was going out of the building."

"Well, forget that, I want you to go out and get that kid back, the murderer kid, before I get any more calls. Understand?" I nodded. "Did you hear about Callahan and the dead Mexican?" I said no, happy to change the subject, but then I had to listen to his version of the incident, which had expanded greatly in the last 12 hours.

After he got to the end and the punchline, I laughed as hard as I could fake it and then beat it for the stairs. Getting my unmarked car out of the lot, I headed for the Palmer home. I was hoping to catch Franklin hiding under the bed, because if he wasn't there, I might have to get a shoe shine. There were reasons I wasn't looking forward to that.

Chapter 10: Lake Front 3600 South

Even though it was day time, and they weren't chasing anyone, all of the emergency vehicles parked along the lake front had their flashing headlights and rotating dome lights on. The police vehicles had blue lights on them now that O. W. Wilson had been brought in to command the police department. He also brought the checkered hat bands with him. No one liked either idea. The hats looked stupid and nobody stopped for a blue light.

There was an ambulance, two squad cars, (one a sergeant's,) and a police wagon. The sergeant had everything in hand, because there was nothing to do.

"Okay, what time was the body found?" That was the first question on the Sergeant's Exam. The patrolman answered, reading from a ten cent spiral notebook.

"He was found by a fisherman at 0730 hours, Sarge." The sergeant let the familiarity go. He looked over to the patrol car where a nervous little black man was sitting in the back worrying that the police might try to pin this incident on him, which happened all the time when the police needed a fall guy for a crime. The sergeant turned to the wagon man.

"Okay, you can take the body to the morgue. Looks like he was walking along the rocks and fell in. Accidental drowning." He'd decided on the cause of death. The biggest part of his job was not raising the crime statistics in his district. The kid was dead, it didn't matter to him what the official cause of death was.

The wagon man, Dougherty, had been on this beat for 25 years. There was nothing he hadn't seen and no atrocity he had not transported but this was the kind of job that he hated most. A little boy, stuck between two big boulders that were lined along Lake Michigan in this area to prevent shore line erosion, his body flapping back and forth with the constant wave motion of the lake.

As his partner approached with the big stretcher that they carried in the back of the wagon, he stepped carefully over the rocks. Dougherty waved him away. Soaked to the skin now, the old timer gently worked the body back and forth until he got the tiny boy out from the clutches of the rocks. He cradled the boy in his arms, giving him one last embrace, the touch of human kindness, the last he would ever receive.

As he approached his partner, Dougherty nodded when he saw that the fire blanket had been laid on top of the stretcher to cover the little boy. "He looks like he's Chinese or something," his partner said. "I wonder why he's so far south. When they want to go fishing the Chinks usually just go east from Chinatown a couple of blocks and they're at the lake?" They covered the boy reverently, Dougherty saying a silent prayer. Then, they secured him in the back of the wagon for the trip to the morgue.

Chapter 11: Curtin gets a shoe shine

The Shine King was an establishment on Indiana Avenue, a few doors south of 42nd Street. Inside was a long narrow space with each wall lined with shoe shine chairs on the top of three wide steps. The middle step held a row of brass foot supports, two for each chair, and the bottom stair was where all the equipment was kept. The shoe shine boys now had access to the customer's feet at a level where they could do the best job. And they did. People came from all over the city to have their shoes shined at the Shine King, or repaired by Sylvester King, the proprietor. He wasn't the boss, Big Mamma was the boss.

When Curtin walked in, Mamma heaved herself up and came around the counter to give him a hug. She didn't do that for anyone but him, and Kelly. The only two white boys to ever shine shoes in her shop.

"Honey Lamb, I'm so happy to see you!" she exclaimed. Then she shouted to Sylvester at the back of the shop where he looked up from behind a mountain of shoes and smiled grimly at Curtin. Curtin didn't really feel sorry for the little overworked man. He made out okay.

Curtin chatted politely with the ageless woman. As far as he could tell, she had always looked the same. A great big woman with a happy smiling face and a wig that was always a little crooked. '*How are the grandchildren?*' '*Fine and dandy*'. '*She was so happy her daughter got out of that trouble she was in'*. (Thanks to Curtin, although Mamma didn't know it.)

Then Curtin lowered his voice and she listened closely. She barked out an order to one of the older boys working on a customer half way down on the left. "Allright? Leave that customer for Sonny Boy and take care of Officer Curtin."

Nobody ever thought of doing anything, but exactly what Mamma ordered. Even the guy who was getting his shoes shined by Allright acted like he didn't even notice the change in personnel. Curtin walked down to an unoccupied chair and climbed up the steps. Allright followed him over and positioned Curtain's feet atop the brass foot rests.

He was over 6 feet tall and easily 225 pounds, no one had ever gotten up the nerve to ask why his name was Allright. The guy had been an enforcer for the second biggest gang on the south side, the Disciples, plus it was impolite. Curtin acted like he knew a hundred people named Allright.

Allright got started working on Curtin's shoes, saddle soap first. He applied polish with his fingertips. He knew something was coming, but was way too cool to worry about it. In his world the kid had creds that were off the scale. He was one of the few who was tough enough to quit the gangs. He had started an accidental family and was pulling five bills a week at the King's, trying to put a life together.

After a few pleasantries Curtin got to the point. "Allright. There was a shooting over on South Park Avenue the other night. Three Rangers were killed. My people have been wondering if it's the start of something that we should be concerned about. You know, to protect the innocent bystanders."

Allright breathed a sigh of relief. He didn't know what he was going to be asked, but being one of the innocent bystanders himself these days, he was expected to protect the other bystanders. Plus Mamma was watching.

"Nah, man," he answered quickly, "Not with the shooting part. That was just family business. The dude's cousin had been stopping by the house when he wasn't home. You know what I'm talkin about?" He didn't wait for the obvious answer to the question.

"So the man puts out the word that the back door man is dead, cousin or no. First, for the disrespect, then for the wife thing. So, instead of doing the smart thing the cousin arms himself, gets two of his boys to back his play, and goes looking for the man to sort of get in the first shot, you understand."

Curtin smiled at Mamma, who was watching the exchange. She turned away to take care of her counter business when she saw Curtin's signal that she had given him the right person.

"Sounds to me like the back door cousin didn't anticipate the man's capabilities," Curtin said to Allright.

"The man kind enough to send you a message *you dead,* when he could have made it a surprise, you see? He's doing you a solid, maybe 'cause he's kinfolk, regardless, the man should have appreciated that gesture and gone the other way. Those other two? They been looking for a place to lay down for a while, now they found it."

"Sounds like a done deal to me," Curtin said.

"It was street justice, that's all. I wouldn't even paid no attention to the story if it weren't for the gun." He snapped the rag across the wing tip, bringing up the high shine.

"Gun?" Curtin said.

"Three people commin at you locked and loaded, how you think you come out of that alive? He had the fire power man." Curtin was leaning into the conversation now, he raised his eyebrows indicating he was very interested.

"A machine gun like. 40, 45 caliber. Fully Automatic. And I heard he's got access to as many as he wants, talks about letting the Panthers have them. I don't like that too much." Now that he was a defender of the people, Allright could see the negative consequences of the black militant groups shooting a bunch of white people, with machine guns, just to make their point.

"How about a name Allright? Unless he's got some cred with you." Curtin wouldn't force him to give up friends, and Allright knew it.

"Dude ain't shit to me. Just a second rate dope dealer. Calls hisself Tombs."

Handing Allright a hundred dollar bill folded up so the numbers couldn't be seen, Curtin climbed down from the high chair. The information was worth the hundred and his shoes looked fabulous.

Chapter 12: Kelly Shine King, no shine

There was a fresh seal on the first floor door. Finding nobody at the Palmer's second floor apartment, I decided to interview a few neighbors and got a feeling that Mrs. Palmer didn't clean houses for a living. Nobody was going to tell a white guy anything for free, especially one that was obviously a cop. Although sticking out like a sore thumb kept me safer in this neighborhood.

It wasn't what people said or didn't say about Lorna Palmer, it was the confused look on their faces when I mentioned her cleaning houses for a living. I thought that it was time for a shoe shine and a little enlightenment.

When I rolled into Mamma's she said, "You just missed your brother." I knew she was talking about Curtin, even though we weren't brothers we grew up together, me practically living at the Curtin's, my mother being dead and my father always working, or drinking, or both.

"Hello Mamma," I said solemnly, going around the counter where no one was allowed and giving her a serious hug. "You look wonderful." I added. She snorted, telling me that I was still the best bull shitter she knew. "I'll catch up with Curtin later, I've got a couple of things I need to talk to you about." The mother hen in her was glowing, seeing two of her *children* coming to her for advice.

"Okay. What's up?" She said, getting that serious look on

her face. I asked her if she knew about the boy, Franklin Palmer, and the death of his downstairs neighbor Sheila. Of course she knew, Mamma knew everything. I just wanted to ease her into it, in case she had other considerations, such as her not wanting to tell me.

"I know him. Ain't nobody seen him though. I let him shine for a few days this summer 'cause his Momma asked me could I give him a job, but he want to be a gangster and you know I don't allow no gang bangin in here." I nodded. She would give anyone a chance, only one per customer. It was a strict rule. I was glad I never violated it.

"You know his mother? Franklin told the detectives that she cleaned houses in Hyde Park, but the neighbors sort of had blank looks on their faces when I asked about that. And that apartment she's living in can't be cheap." Six rooms for two people?

"That's 'cause she works for the Policy Man. She don't get her hands dirty, no. In fact, she's got somebody cleaning her house." She laughed. "Nobody gonna tell you nothing, cause nobody wants to get the Policy Man mad at them. It could cause your dreams to go away."

Policy was a form of lottery gambling that was unique to the black neighborhoods in Chicago. The Vice guys picked up the policy runners, and confiscated their printing presses on a regular basis, but there was too much money in it to ever eradicate. The Vice guys were the only ones who dressed better, and drove bigger cars, than Homicide Detectives.

The Policy Man could be found in the poorest

neighborhoods of the south side, or west side, carrying his Dream Book with a big fat rubber band around it locking in secrets. Word would spread that he was on the block and people would come out and make bets on tomorrow's policy wheel numbers. You could bet as little as five cents. He also handed out little slips of paper, which were printed on the little portable printing presses, giving yesterday's winning numbers. Many a grocery list was written on the back of a losing policy slip.

The games had different names. "*Win, Place and Show*" was the most popular. There were three, four and five numbers drawn for each game. Each had different odds, like a horse race. Everybody played his birthday or a special number. Everybody had dreams.

The Policy Man was there to fulfill dreams. If you had a dream about being chased by a lion the Policy Man would look it up in his *Dream Book* and there would be corresponding numbers that you would bet. He would record your bet. Bet a nickel. If your numbers came up, you would collect a quarter the next day. Five to one payoff wasn't bad in any game.

"Looks like I'm going to have more work getting that kid back." I said. If the policy people were involved they could hide the boy for her and I'd never find him. They weren't gangsters really, in fact the real Mob didn't bother collecting a share of the games. It was too much trouble chasing the money around. Black people didn't care if you were the Mafia or not. White was white and they had been learning how to avoid them in America for four hundred years now.

"Did that boy really stab that poor girl to death? Lord bless her and take her to His bosom." Mamma was appalled by the violence she saw every day. She knew she wasn't going to pray it away.

"Yes, Mamma, he did." I left it there. I wanted to sugar coat it for her a little but there was no lying to her. The details would only have made it worse. She sensed it and didn't ask more.

"I would have said it was that scoundrel Johnny Slater. He is a no good." She was ready to go on him so I shook my head and changed the subject. Johnny Slater was just another pimp and not a good one, if there was such a thing. But that was also a Vice Control Division matter and not my job.

"The other thing I wanted to ask you about Mamma, is a little Vietnamese boy." I shouldn't have asked. I needed to get going, I wasn't going to find Franklin in the shoe shine shop. "Did you see a little white boy around yesterday?"

"Sho did." She smiled, noticing that I had changed the topic. "He was walking around all scared like a little rabbit. I sent one of the boys to bring him in here but he bolted and ran away."

"Well, they caught him. The report said that Mr. Washington found the boy and turned him in to the Youth Division."

"Is he all right now? Did you find out where he belongs?" She asked, I didn't want to tell her about the bruises on the boy so I told her he was all right. Stretching it a little bit.

"He's being taken care of." I thought of Nurse Miller and

was sure nobody was abusing him. "I'd better find Mr. Washington and ask him." I remembered dreading coming to talk to him when I saw his name on the case report that had accompanied Poc.

Patrolman, First Class, Cecil Washington was the boss of Indiana Avenue. It could have been any street. When he walked out of the 2nd District station house on 42nd and Indiana, people watched to see which way he turned and the word would spread. In one direction everybody relaxed, in the other direction people ran for their lives if they been warned.

If you were a known criminal, or even suspected in his estimation, you got one warning. "*I don't want to see you again. If I do you gonna be dead.*" It was a simple statement and people defied him at their own peril. He had backed up that threat many times. Whenever he found someone who he had warned violating his order he would just shoot the guy, then he would call a wagon, send the body to the morgue and write all the reports himself. No one ever questioned a word.

This was a black neighborhood, and the police officers were black. They took care of their own business, especially Cecil Washington. One of the legendary stories about him told of three guys who had robbed the First National Bank on 47th and Indiana. They had the misfortune of doing it when Mr. Washington was walking down the street. When they came out of the bank, cash and guns in hand, he just stood there in the street, pulled his two silver .38 caliber revolvers and started exchanging shots with the three robbers.

One of them shot off his hat, but Cecil Washington was

a dead shot, he killed all three of the bank robbers while bullets were flying around him. After he holstered his smoking revolvers he picked up his hat, he put his finger through the hole shaking his head sadly, he was just getting that hat broken in right.

At the curb to his right, he noticed a 1962 Chevy Impala, running, with a nervous guy sitting behind the wheel. He was looking straight ahead. Everybody on the street was looking at Washington but this guy. Mr. Washington put a round in the side of the guy's head and walked up to the restaurant he had been on his way to for his lunch, hat in hand. They never proved that guy in the Impala was the get-a-way driver, but nobody said he wasn't.

"Well, there he is." Mamma pointed across the street to the 2nd District Police Station, where a large black man was casually walking down the stairs. He was all decked out in a tailored uniform, blue poplin shirt, pin straight crease in his pants with white piping running down the sides, Chicago Police Star pinned over his heart. He was wearing a one piece black leather gun belt with two revolvers so shiny I could see them gleam from across the street.

I didn't have to find Mr. Washington, he was about to find me. He started across the street angling directly for the Shine King. Cars screeched to a stop, parting like the Red Sea for him to cross. Curtin and I had called him Mr. Washington when we were kids and were still afraid to get any more personal even though we were all on the same police force now, well, not the same.

When he came into the shop taking off his hat, the little bell over the door tinkled. His hair was black and slicked flat to his head like Cab Calloway. He also had a pencil thin mustache making him sort of look like Calloway. I think he privately liked the comparison.

"Miss Abigail." He bowed an inch in her direction.

"Hello, Cecil." She answered politely. They'd known each other since the Stone Age. No one called her Miss Abigail. I didn't even know she had a first name, and no one I knew had ever called him Cecil, to his face that is.

"Hello, Boy," he said to me acting like he had just noticed me standing there. He noticed everything, that's why he had lasted so long on the street.

"Mr. Washington." I answered politely.

"What brings you to the ghetto?" He didn't think this was a ghetto, but he thought I thought so. "That little Chinese boy?" He asked, looking closely at me.

I couldn't hide the shock on my face. He didn't wait. It was unnecessary for me to answer the question.

He pulled his six shooters out of their holsters and twirled them like Hoot Gibson, deftly setting them on the counter, pointing the barrels towards himself, after the little display. That was when I noticed that all the shoe shine boys had been waiting for him to do his stuff. The looks on their faces were pure astonishment and admiration. I was impressed too!

He took off his gun belt and handed it to the nearest boy saying, "Can you polish up my gun belt, Boy?"

The boy took the belt reverently and turned to his bench. I

realized that it was his turn to get this honor, as the other boys looked over his shoulder giving him pointers of how to apply the black Kiwi polish and warning him to be careful with those bullets. The back of the belt had enough bullets lined up in little loops to kill everyone on Indiana Avenue. I only had five in my snub nose.

He turned to me. "How's that brother of yours, the one that's always getting into trouble."

"He's okay. Mamma said he was just in here." I saw that I shouldn't have said that, Washington looked out the window like Curtin was on the street up to some mischief like in the old days.

To distract him I said. "Although he's getting better at getting out of trouble." Reading my mind again, Washington laughed and changed the subject.

"I don't know nothing about that little boy other than he was lost and scared. He wouldn't say a word. He kept looking around for someone though, someone he was afraid of, I'd say. He might have run away from somewhere. Although I can't think of any place where white children live around here. I couldn't do anything with him so I brought him over to the Area."

"We think he's Vietnamese." I lowered my voice. "And someone has been beating him. Did you notice anything like that, Mr. Washington?"

"Vietnam, you say....hum....yes I did see some little marks on his skin. You say that was from a beating?" I nodded.

"Well, I want to know what becomes of that boy. You

understand?" His look said I had better, so I nodded, he doubled down. "God pushed that child into my arms and I'm not going to push him away. You understand me, Boy?"

"Yes, Sir." I said, promising. A nod wasn't good enough, apparently. Mamma could call him Cecil, everybody else called him *Sir*.

Chapter 13: The Home

"Drowned? Saints preserve us!" When he was really stressed, his brogue was very pronounced. "How in the hell do you know that?"

"Well, when you said to check around, without letting on that we were looking for them, I called over to the morgue."

"The morgue! Are you insane?"

"I didn't tell them who I was, I just asked if they had any little oriental boys."

"And they just told you that they had our boys there in the morgue."

"The person who answered the phone didn't ask my name and didn't give his when he answered. He just said "*Morgue*", but when I asked him he said that he had a little Chinese boy that had been fished out of the lake just to the south of here. It has to be one of them." He thought that was pretty clever work. He glanced out the window at the blue panorama of Lake Michigan, from here it looked like an ocean.

"Did he say anything about the other one?"

"Uh, he said he had one boy. I didn't want to ask about the other one. He wouldn't have known anything any way, unless the other one was dead too."

"That would solve our problem though," he mused. "This is also going to be very costly. Well, get your ass out there and find the other one. Drowned, poor boy, this is terrible, terrible."

"What about the one in the morgue?" He might as well ask a stupid question, before being blamed for results that were out of his control.

"You'll have to report him missing. Damn you! We need to get that body out of the morgue." He was furious. "But wait a day or so, maybe the other one will turn up."

Chapter 14: Cook County Morgue

"Morgue? Why do I have to go to the morgue?" I've hated the morgue since they made us go there to observe an autopsy when we were in the police academy. Of course, Curtin loved it and used to go there all the time. He probably still does.

"Because your kid is in the morgue, Kelly. That's why."

"What kid? Franklin Palmer?" That would save society a lot of money over the coming years.

"No, the Chink." Toolis was raising his voice again and he got a coughing fit.

I started talking to give him time to recover. "Are you telling me that both of the kids that I brought to the Audy home escaped?"

"I'm telling you to go and find out who's in the morgue. There's either one or two missing Chink's now. You're losing these kids, Kelly, not me, first the murderer and now...." He started choking and I headed for the stairs before I was a witness to a heart attack.

The first thing I did, which surprised me that no one had already done, was to call the Audy Home and ask if Poc was still there. Nobody wanted to tell me anything which was par for the course but I persisted and got an orderly to physically go to his room to verify that he was still there.

I could have talked my way out of it at that point, but I let curiosity get the better of me, again.

The morgue was on the near north side close to Cook County Hospital so they wouldn't have to transport the bodies too far when they steadily rolled out of the County's back door. The entrance was at the side of a long shipping dock, not shipping actually, more unshipping.

The wagons and ambulances would back up to the dock, maybe wide enough for three vehicles, and unload their grizzly cargos. If you died quietly in your bed surrounded by loved ones, the funeral director sent a hearse to your home to collect you and bring you to the funeral parlor.

If you were found dead on the streets of Chicago, maybe shot or run over, or if you drowned in the lake, as it turned out, you ended up in a drawer in the morgue.

The guy who took me back to the refrigerator room was the definition of a ghoul. When I walked in to the reception area, he was eating a sandwich while wearing rubber gloves. I couldn't figure that out and didn't want to know.

He wore a green smock, with splashes of dead people all over it, which looked like he only changed it monthly. When he opened the big door I could see bodies on gurneys packed into the room like sardines. The wall of drawers in the back must have been full of customers too.

"Just a minute," he said. "The kid's in the back there. I've got to do a little re-ranging so I can get him out."

I was gagging on the smells, not just death and decay. Every nasty smell that was available to the nose seemed to be coming out of that room, while the worker pulled one gurney after the other out and rolled them into the hallway to get to the one he wanted. The ice cold air that rushed out with the stench gave me a shiver.

There were no wrappings on the bodies, no sheets covering them. Everyone that he pushed past me was a different story. Gray colored, mouths gaping, eyes staring vacantly. The last body he pulled out, before the little boy, was burned to a crisp, you couldn't even tell if it was male or female.

It had *stomach-turning-inside-out* stench coming from it. I realized that the ghoul had done this on purpose to fuck with me. Another reason I hated coming to the morgue, the living people were just as disgusting as the dead. I did manage to disappoint him and not toss my cookies.

As soon as I saw the boy, I knew there was a problem. He had a little white tag tied to his toe. All it said was *Unknown*.

I knew the victim wasn't going to be Poc, but there were glaring similarities. He was about the same age and looked like he was Vietnamese. His thick black hair was cut in the same soup bowl style as Poc's. And there were hundreds of small, round, black and blue bruises on his tiny body.

Chapter 15: Lake Front 3900 South

I got the ghoul guy to give me a copy of the Hospital Report on the kid. The wagon men had to take him to a hospital to have him officially pronounced dead before the morgue would take the body. On the report it also stated where they had found the boy.

I took a ride south to 39th Street on Lake Shore Drive, exited the Drive and went over the bridge to the lake front. There was parking but no beach along this stretch of Lake Michigan. I parked and walked a block or so south on the giant square rocks that were haphazardly piled along the shoreline as far as you could see in either direction.

It didn't take me long to find where the boy had been found in the lake. There were no signs of police presence but the tire tracks and muddy foot prints on the rocks led me to the approximate area where they had pulled the boy from the lake.

I could have asked for a meet with Dougherty the wagon man but it didn't matter. I didn't need to know where he had been found exactly, I needed to find the place where he went into the water. I searched the entire area. There was nothing.

After I had gone back and forth in both directions, I ended up where I had started. I paused for a moment looking down into the murky water that washed over the rocks with regular cadence. A little boy like Poc had drowned there. Why? Where had he come from? Just then I looked over to the winding sidewalk that ran along the parkway for bikes and pedestrians, and saw Franklin Palmer.

He took one look at me and bolted, heading south along the path. I ran after him. You get a lot of exercise being a Youth Officer. You're always chasing some kid somewhere, school truants, graffiti artists, or just general business, like murder in Franklin's case.

He was fast and lengthened the distance between us. His problem was that he couldn't get off this part of the lake front until he got to 47th Street unless he ran across six lanes of traffic. He didn't know it, but if he had the nerve to do that he wouldn't have to worry about me chasing him across the Drive.

Slow and steady, that was my running style. I wasn't fast, but I could go the distance. He looked over his shoulder and saw that I was closing, so he tried to speed it up, but just ran out of gas sooner. I caught him after about half a mile. He was as winded as I was, and didn't resist. The only problem was that he wasn't Franklin Palmer.

Same height, weight, curly hair style. From where I had been when I first saw him, it looked like Franklin Palmer. I guess that I just assumed it was him when he ran.

"Why did you run?" I had his hands cuffed behind him while I was going through his pockets.

"'Cause you was chasing me." It made sense to him.

In his back pocket I found a plastic bag. That was it, he was selling pot. After chasing him all over the lake front, I wasn't about to let him go even though reefer wasn't a big deal these days. I took the bag and started opening it. There was no dope in the bag, it was just a greasy plastic bag that was all balled up in his pocket.

"What the hell is this?" I asked him holding the greasy thing out to him.

"That's my Gerri Curl bag, man." It was the bag he put over his head to do whatever this goop I had all over my hands was supposed to do to his hair to make it curly and shiny. I took the cuffs off him and told him to beat it. Then I went and washed my hands in the lake, probably polluting the whole thing.

Chapter 16: Audy Home

Nurse Katherine L. Miller, former Captain Miller US Army Medical Corps, took the job as a nurse at the Audy Home in Chicago after her tours in Vietnam. She was weary of seeing young men wounded on the battle field and having to sew and patch them together like garments in order to try and save lives that should not have been in jeopardy.

She didn't expect to find any AK 47 wounds coming in to her infirmary. And she didn't. What she did see was worse in many ways, but she was a nurse to her core. She had taken an oath just like doctors. She cared for these children, regardless of their trauma.

Poc had been sexually abused; she was sure of it. He wouldn't let her examine him though, and she wasn't going to press the issue, at least not now. The boy was eating like a horse and even smiling occasionally. The children that came into the Audy Home were often physically abused, neglected, dirty and unable to care for themselves. Some have never brushed their teeth in their entire lives.

But the ones that were sexually abused were the saddest. They were harmed on the inside. Their innocence was ripped away from them. The files she read told the horrific tales in frank medical terms, but the reality of what the victims suffered was never addressed.

It seemed that people didn't want to think about the horror children suffered at the hands of sexual predators, not because they were monsters themselves, surely, but because it was too difficult to imagine for a normal human being.

"Miz Miller," She put Poc's thin file down and turned to the door. The orderly had put his head in. "You have a phone call, Ma'am." He pointed at the blinking light on the black standard office phone. She pushed the button and picked up the receiver.

"Hello."

"Hello. Uh, Nurse Miller?" She knew who it was before he identified himself.

"Cut the comedy *Officer* Kelly. What do you want?" She was immediately sorry she had jumped on him. He was trying to help the boy. It was just her frustration. "Sorry, Kelly, what can I do for you? Poc is doing okay, but in a way I'm glad you called..."

"I didn't call about him." He cut her short.

"Oh? What did you call about?"

He hesitated before speaking, "They found a little boy drowned in Lake Michigan." Kay didn't say anything. She didn't realize that she was holding her breath.

"There has to be a connection to Poc. This boy looks to be Vietnamese and has the same haircut as Poc." She knew there was more and waited. He waited too, and she still didn't say anything. She waited him out.

"And he has the same marks on him as Poc." Kay closed her eyes tightly, trying to squeeze out the picture that had come to mind.

"Oh, my God!" she whispered. Glancing down at Poc's file she couldn't control the emotions that came over her when she realized that he was not alone in his plight, that he was the lucky one. Tears welled in her eyes.

"I'm sorry." Kelly said, sensing that she was upset even over the phone.

She almost lashed out at him again. What was he apologizing for? She caught herself. "What are we going to do?" Her voice cracked a little. She felt so helpless.

"Has anyone contacted the Audy Home asking about Poc?" At least he had a question.

"No."

"Uh...okay." It seemed he couldn't think of anything else to say.

"I'm fairly certain that Poc has been sexually abused," she said.

"What!" That got his brain working.

"I think he was sexually abused," she repeated. "He won't let me examine him, but from the way he reacted when I tried, I'm sure he is suffering from some kind of anal problem. Probably a fissure from sodomy penetration."

"Poor little guy." Kelly sounded genuinely concerned.

"Well?" She said, implying that if he was going to do something helpful, now was the time.

"Well, okay. Let's see. Send him over to the hospital. Get a doctor to look at him. After we have a doctor's opinion....we uh...take it from there." She told him she wasn't going to get the authorization to do that.

"Well, has he said anything that will help us find out where he's been or who has been abusing these children?" Another part of the problem.

"He hasn't said a word, other than his name, although he understands and obeys all commands. But I can't just send him to the hospital on a hunch. I can't even justify taking him out of the facility or make an official statement like that unless I have more facts than I have now." She was so frustrated.

"Well, I don't need any more facts, I'm the damn police. I'll be right over to get him and take him to the hospital. Don't worry!"

"*Don't worry.*" She didn't like the sound of that at all.

Chapter 17: Audy Home Director's Office

When I arrived at the Audy Home, I was left outside on the stoop after I buzzed the intercom and gave my name. I had completely forgotten that these people were blaming me for letting Franklin Palmer escape from their jail.

It seemed like an eternity but was only half that long before someone finally buzzed the door lock. I walked in to the vestibule up the stairs knocking on the other door. It didn't buzz open automatically when I approached like it had the last time.

Looking back at the space in the vestibule I thought to myself, "*How in the hell did that kid supposedly slip past two locked doors walking closely behind me?*" He didn't. That's how.

They made me wait for the other door too. Then it was opened from the inside by a security guard. He was the one that had been on the desk when I brought Franklin and Poc in. It didn't take but a glance to realize that he was involved somehow. He was paying attention to me now, giving me the "*Wolf Cookie*" look. It might scare these children, but it only pissed me off. He was a big bastard though.

"Doctor Bagdonas says he wants to see you," he said, as though he was looking for me to resist his order.

Louis Bagdonas was the Director of the Audy Home, which was a big political job, but I didn't answer to him. I thought of telling the guard, Simmons on the name plate, to shove it, but I wanted to know more about the Franklin Palmer thing anyway. I followed him down the hall to a big wooden door.

The Director's office looked like every warden's office in any prison in the country. Pictures of his charges digging vegetables in the yard or holding up medals won at some fake institutional sporting event. Then, there was a plethora of pictures with every politician he could get a photo with. Bagdonas, or should I say *Doctor Bagdonas*, was sitting behind a brass plate with his name on it that sat on a desk so big it made him look smaller.

He had bushy hair, which was hiding a receding hairline, and a walrus mustache. "Mr. Kelly, I'd like to talk to you about the boy Franklin Palmer……. who escaped the other night." The word *escape* was like vinegar in his mouth.

Simmons had stayed in the room when he brought me in, making me think that Bagdonas was complicit in trying to blame me for the escape. It didn't bother me to say *escape*.

"Right, the escape." I let it hang, glancing back at Simmons, who was trying to intimidate me with his huge presence now. I almost laughed thinking how fast I could wipe that scowl off of his face. But I was in a hurry and decided to be frank with the guy.

"I brought two boys in the other night. Franklin Palmer, I took over to the detention side and signed him in. After that I took the other boy to the other side where he was checked out by the nurse. That's why I'm here. To take that boy to the hospital because he may have been sexually abused." Bagdonas' jaw was hanging open, I didn't give him a chance to think, much less talk.

"Now, *you* lost Franklin Palmer, Doctor. I don't know how and I wouldn't care other than you loosed a murderer back onto the streets of Chicago. Instead of *talking* to me about it you should start looking around here if you want to know how he escaped." I had his attention now.

"I would start by asking *Officer* Simmons if he saw Palmer walk out behind me. He was sitting right there at the desk when I left, by myself." He had a round pudgy face and it was red as a tomato. First he wanted to talk to me and now he couldn't talk.

"Okay, so '*You wanted to talk to me?*' Doctor, you just did. You can make up any shit you want about how the kid got out. But I'd leave me out of it, if I were you." Bagdonas was so furious I thought he was going to sic his body guard on me, but he just stood there and stammered. He wisely kept the big desk between us. I didn't care what he had to say.

I turned and walked out of his office. I tensed, waiting for Simmons to walk out after me. I was thinking of several things that I would like to do to him, but he stayed. I went straight to the infirmary. Nurse Miller was there and so was Poc, who was looking much better wearing clean clothes and a clean face. He wasn't smiling though. I smiled at him.

"Kelly, can you really do this? Just take him out on your own authority."

"Are you willing to back up your statement regarding his possible sexual abuse?"

"Absolutely!"

"After my little meeting with Director Doctor Bagdonas just now, wild horses couldn't stop me." She smiled. It was a pretty one, first I'd seen.

She explained to Poc that he should go with me and he didn't resist, although he wasn't happy about it. I watched him like a hawk, my hand constantly on his shoulder. Simmons was back at his desk but just stared at me when we walked past. He didn't try to stop us or even say a word. Too late, I had it saved for that asshole. If he told Bagdonas that the kid walked out behind me, he was a liar. That was a crime in my book.

Chapter 18: The Home

"He's at whose home?"

"The Audy Home. It's a juvenile detention center."

"What do we have to do to get him out?"

"Apparently just go there and sign him out. We'll have to file a missing person report and admit that the boy in the morgue was one of two boys who *wandered away*. One tragically dying while playing along the lake front, the other rescued by the police and held in custody until they found his guardians. Namely, us."

"You have it all figured out, do you?"

"Well, I found him and was just thinking about how...."

"Shut up! You idiot! If there is any explanation to be made, I will make it. I will go to this Audy Home and you will go to the police and report the *wandering youths* and then go and get that body from the morgue."

"What should I do with it?"

"Take it to the facility on Halsted. Tell Goddard to have his GR guys take care of it. Tell them I said I need it done immediately. Then when you go back to Vietnam you can take the ashes with you and spread them in a river or something. Remember to take a lot of pictures," he said, always thinking.

"Uh.....now's not the best time to be over there....the Viet

Cong have been swarming all over the country side, we have......"

"I know what we have! A shortage! That's what! We need more boys, the two we planned to lose and the two you lost. You want a choice, fine. The Viet Cong.......or me?"

"I'll start packing." Putting it that way, it was no contest. At least the VC would kill you quicker.

"And have my car brought around. Make sure the driver knows where the hell we're going." Maybe this idiot will do me the courtesy of getting killed by the Viet Cong and save me the trouble, he mused. His dreams were big and satisfying.

Chapter 19: Cook County Hospital

Arriving at the Cook County Hospital, I parked the unmarked car right in front and took Poc into the Emergency Room. The reception area was big enough to play a basketball game in there, with rows and rows of chairs, all with arms so the patients couldn't lay down.

It was said to be the largest hospital in the world, or they treated more people than any hospital in the world. I couldn't remember which one. Whatever, I knew that they were the real pros here, just by reason of the volume of people and trauma they saw. Doctors who did their residency at County were sought after across the country.

The place was awesome. I'd bet they could take a bullet out of you in the waiting room. Did they cover everything imaginable? What have you got? Leprosy? No problem. They had two cases last year.

I went up to the counter, holding Poc gently by the shoulder, checked in and told the desk clerk what I needed. I showed her my badge. She wasn't impressed. I asked her if any of the doctors spoke Vietnamese and she looked at me like I was speaking Vietnamese.

There were about fifty people ahead of us so I leaned on the counter and sweet talked her until she got tired of the bullshit and agreed to go ask a doctor if I was worth going to the head of the line. I didn't want Poc around other people, sick or not, so we moved out into the hall where I could see the clerk and she could see me, although she wasn't looking.

I wished that I could find a doctor that spoke Vietnamese. That would work perfectly for me. While we were standing there people of all kinds were coming and going. Poc and I just watched the people and enjoyed the show. Down the hall, I noticed a pregnant woman looking into the maternity clinic through the glass windows in the double doors. There were a lot of pregnant women going in and out but she just stood there in front of the doors as though she was looking for someone.

She looked very pregnant, the baby bump big and low. Then a funny thing happened. A nurse came out of the clinic, pushing the door hard and it hit the woman right in her stomach. The nurse was mortified when she realized what she had accidentally done, but the woman brushed it off, said she was all right and walked away down the corridor. The strange thing was that she didn't clutch her stomach when it was struck, she didn't even touch it or rub the spot where she was hit.

Just then I realized that someone was speaking to Poc. It was the janitor, pushing a cart with supplies and a garbage can with mops and brooms sticking out of the top. As it turned out not only was he Vietnamese, he was also a doctor, or had been one in Vietnam at least. In Chicago, he was the janitor. I didn't care. His name plate said Nguyen, I introduced myself and quickly told him what I needed. He listened solemnly, once a doctor always a doctor.

Chapter 20: Audy Home Director's Office

When the intercom on her desk buzzed Kay almost jumped out of her seat. She had been waiting for the phone to ring, hoping to hear from Kelly. The intercom was a different machine and had a piercing sound. "Yes." She said pressing the talk button.

"Miss Miller, could you please come into my office?" It was Director Bagdonas and he rarely asked her anything, she had only had the honor of being in his office once.

When she walked into the office, holding the big wooden door to close it softly, she was surprised to see another person in the office. It was a priest. He was sitting in one of the button tufted leather chairs that flanked the big desk that Bagdonas sat behind. Even sitting down, wearing a coarse brown robe and sandals, the priest was an impressive man. He had to be over six feet tall, he filled the chair. His hair was silver but his face wasn't lined with age. Movie star handsome in her opinion. He rose to take her hand, towering over her, when Bagdonas introduced him.

"Miss Miller is our chief medical officer." Bagdonas was fawning all over this guy, probably looking forward to a picture with the priest for his wall.

"Miss Miller, this is Father Antonin Brown. He is the Director of *Father Brown's Home for Boys*. It seems that our little Vietnamese boy belongs to him."

Kay had forced a smile that was wiped off her face when the priest stood up. She stood there in shock, with the priest gently holding her hand. The first thing she noticed about the priest was a curious circular scar in the palm of his hand, like a puncture wound, the second thing was around his waist cinching his robe.

His warm friendly eyes abruptly changed when he noticed where her glance had gone, she was in danger from this man because of what she had seen. Kay could see the cold threat in those grey eyes.

What she saw that stunned her was the large rosary that Father Brown's Religious Order wore as a belt for their long robes. He let go of her hand and turned back to the desk as Bagdonas continued talking, not noticing the exchange between the priest and the nurse.

"Miss Miller, I want you to call the County hospital and find that policeman, Kelly, and tell him to stay where he is and Father Brown will be kind enough to pick the boy up from him at the hospital." Apparently the question of the boy's physical and sexual assault was not an issue.

When she didn't respond he said, testily, "Can you do that? Miss Miller?"

"Uh yes, Doctor, I'll call there and give him the message." She turned and headed for the door, avoiding looking at the priest. Bagdonas made all the staff call him Doctor, implying that he was an M.D., even though he actually had a PHD in Social Science and couldn't really doctor a cat.

Chapter 21: Cook County Hospital, a call for help

"Hey!" The emergency room clerk was standing right behind me in the hallway. And she wasn't smiling. "You have a phone call, if your name is Kelly."

"Yea, Kelly, I'll be right there." That didn't make her happy either, she just walked away. I looked at Doctor Nguyen not wanting to interrupt his conversation with Poc. The boy had been talking nonstop since Nguyen had established a limited pattern of trust with the boy. Nguyen looked back at me and nodded imperceptibly, the boy was okay now but admitted to being a victim of sexual abuse.

The clerk gestured to the phone that was off the hook lying on the counter top. I picked it up and said, "Hello".

"Kelly, oh thank God I found you." She was always saying things that I wished she meant differently.

"What?"

"There's a man here to pick up Poc." I could tell that wasn't a good thing. "He's a priest."

I didn't know what to think of that. "A priest? What could he have to do with Poc?"

"He has a home for boys, *Father Brown's Home for Boys*," she said sarcastically.

"How did he even know the boy was at the Audy Home?"

"I don't know Kelly, and I don't care. You have to do something!" Here we go again what?

"Kelly, he has a long rosary that he wears around his waist that hangs down. Little round beads strung on a cord." She let it sink in.

"Holy Shit!" I looked over to where Doctor Nguyen was watching Poc for me. He was making the boy laugh.

"Stall him as long as you can, I'll think of something."

"Stall him? Doctor Bags has already called me twice on the intercom."

"Tell him that you left a message at the Emergency Room desk. Tell them that the clerk told you I was there but was not around the desk area. And that she would give me the message."

"Okay, but you have to think of something quick. Bags is showing him around the facility but the priest isn't going to tolerate Bags for too long." She hung up, out of things to ask for.

I grabbed the base of the phone and scrunched my nose at the clerk when she gave me an annoyed look. I dialed a number that I had known all my life.

"Hello."

"Curtin?" The voice was a little off.

"No, this is Michael. Who's this?"

I was relieved, a plan was forming in my head, if I could just get him to go along with it.

"Mickey, it's Jim Kelly. I'm glad you're there. I need a priest."

"Not for Last Rites, I hope?" Michael laughed and I told him what I needed, and why. He stopped laughing.

Doctor Nguyen's diagnosis that the boy was okay *now*, would have to hold us. I didn't want to be here when Father Brown arrived, so we boogied without being seen by the ER Staff. Considering how many people were in the waiting room, I doubted they would miss us.

When we got out front, my squad was blocked by a CTA bus loading passengers. As we waited along with the bus driver for his passengers to climb aboard, I noticed one of them was the pregnant girl from the clinic who had gotten wacked by the swinging door. She hopped up the stairs of the bus like it was nothing.

I thought that a woman who was that pregnant would at least have held on to the rails and taken her time getting on the bus. I would have chalked it up to youth, but she wasn't that young. The bus driver closed the door and pulled away in a cloud of diesel smoke.

There was a ticket on my windshield and I took it off and threw it into the glove compartment with the rest. It was obviously a police vehicle, just like the blue and white ones but solid blue with no dome light. Some wise guy foot patrolman was trying to send me a message, I had a finger gesture I'd like to answer him with, but he wasn't around. We hopped in the car and headed south hoping for a miracle.

Chapter 22: Cook County Hospital

Father Brown swept into the County Hospital like he was Jesus coming to heal the sick. He even blessed a few people that looked like they needed it. He went to the desk and inquired where he might find Officer Kelly and was handed a note by the clerk. Nguyen had a great relationship with all of the staff and had convinced her to help out and play along with Kelly's scheme.

The note stated that Officer Kelly had taken the boy to the Area 3 Youth Division for processing. Brown didn't know what processing could have taken precedence over his order to remain at the hospital until he arrived, but when he got finished with that Kelly officer, that flatfoot would be sweeping the streets for a living and whatever the *Third Area* was would be a pile of rubble when he was through. '*Processing*', he didn't like that word, there may have to be more cleaning done, besides the cop and the nurse.

Chapter 23: Area 3 the Switch

When I rushed into the Area lobby with Poc, I went right to the desk and told Flynn that a priest was coming in to pick up the kid and to send him right upstairs. He acted like that wasn't part of his job.

I took the boy up to my office, which was just a big room with a lot of old wooden desks, and we waited. I tried to tell Poc that everything would be all right, but I wasn't sure myself and it showed.

"Oh, so you found him." Toolis came out of his office. He had a real office, although it had a door that didn't close.

"I thought he was dead," he said looking at Poc.

"Ix-ney on the ed-day, will you, Sarge." I hadn't said anything about the other boy and didn't want to have to start explaining now. Lighting a Lucky Strike, Toolis took the hint and walked back in his office.

Down in the lobby a priest came through the doors, dressed in sandals, and long brown robes, tied with the knotted double cord that Franciscans wore. He had his cowl turned up obscuring his face. Flynn called out right away, telling him that he should go up to the second floor and turn right. It never hurt to do a little favor for a priest. The priest waved and started up the stairs.

When he came into the office Mickey Curtin pulled the

cowl down showing his broad smile, but Poc went into a little panic and tried to hide behind me. Mickey came over and started to talk to the boy softly, in Vietnamese. Everybody could speak Vietnamese, but me, it seemed. We didn't have much time and I mentioned it to Mickey.

He looked up at me and smiled. "We're going to be okay, Jimmy. I'm glad I remembered the words for chocolate cake though. We'll see you at the house."

Poc took Mickey's hand and they went down the back stairs to avoid the other priest if he happened to be coming up from the lobby. I also thought I had better learn how to say chocolate cake in as many languages as possible.

I couldn't believe that the promise of chocolate cake was all it took to get Poc to trust Mickey. I knew it wasn't really, Mickey had a way with people. The boy trusted him almost from the smile. So did I.

Chapter 24: Area 3 Youth Office

Father Brown swept into the 3rd Area lobby with the same swagger he had at the County Hospital. He didn't bless anyone, however, he was in the opposite mood. He was furious and intended to take every inch of hide off of that little heathen Poc.

He walked toward the desk and Flynn looked up from the log book. "Second floor, Father, turn right." He pointed up and Brown changed directions heading for the stairs. When he reached the second floor, he saw the sign for the Youth Division to his right and marched boldly through the door.

"Are you Kelly?" He demanded of the first person he saw, it was Frankie Bartuca, who laughed then pointed over at Kelly who was as different looking as night and day from the dark Italian.

"Officer Kelly?" Brown scrutinized Kelly closely, not wanting to forget a line of his face.

"Yes, Father. What can I do for you?" Kelly was sitting at a desk with an Olympic typewriter in front of him. There was a sheaf of papers wound through the roller. Six report forms and six carbons. You had to really bang hard on the keys to push the imprint of the letters through twelve sheets of paper. The only Xerox copy machine the Department had was at 11th and State.

"You can release my boy to me and allow me to be on my

way." Brown would take care of these people in his own good time. What was important now was getting the boy back and limiting the exposure. This was costing him a fortune.

He took a moment to pray that Halloran was killed in Vietnam when he sent him back there on the next plane. He knew that if the Communists captured a priest, or anyone who was spreading Christian teachings, they were extra creative in how those people were dispatched.

"What boy?" Kelly asked.

"The Vietnamese boy that you brought here from the hospital against my specific instructions. He is an orphan and is being cared for at my home for boys."

"What home is that, Father?"

"Are you trying to get cute with me son? If so, I will immediately deal with your superior." To calm himself he said a silent prayer that this would be over soon. Not wanting to wait for the superior he capitulated. "Father Brown's Home for Boys."

"Oh, that boy, he's gone. They picked him up already."

"What!" Brown bellowed. "Who picked him up?"

"Father Brown."

"I'm Father Brown!!"

Sergeant Toolis came out of his office. He quickly threw his cigarette on the floor, grinding it into the old hardwood, when he saw the tall, silver haired priest screaming in the middle of his squad room.

"You're Father Brown? Then who was the other priest?" Kelly asked.

"That's what I want to know!" Waves of rage were coming off Brown. "I told you to wait at the hospital and when I arrive there I am given a note." He had a crumpled piece of paper in his hand.

"A note! Directing *me* come to this place to pick up my boy. Now you say he was picked up by another priest. That's preposterous! There is no other priest. No other Father Brown. You people are hiding that child and I am going to call the Mayor and have you all fired! Fired, do you hear?"

Toolis believed in being respectful but threatening him with the Mayor had the opposite effect. "Look Padre. There must be some mistake. One of your guys was just here and picked the kid up. Why don't you call the rectory and see. He's probably there already." Toolis gestured toward the phone.

Brown calmed himself. "What is your name, sir?"

"Toolis, Sergeant Thomas J. Toolis."

"Sergeant Toolis, are you telling me that you saw a priest come into this room, and take that child away."

"That's what I'm telling you."

Brown looked over at Bartuca, then at Kelly. Both nodded.

Chapter 25: Area 3 Lobby

When Brown turned and left the room in a huff, I was sure there was more to come so I got up from my fake report that I wasn't typing, and followed. He went down to the lobby and stood in front of the high metal counter across from Sergeant Kern, who was on the phone. Brown glared at Kern until he cut the call short and asked Brown what he wanted.

"I would like to use your phone please." Reasonable request, Kern turned the instrument around so the priest could have access. The desk phone would give him no privacy, only going as far from the desk as the length of the curly cord. There was a phone booth in the corner, as there was in every police station, but Brown apparently didn't want privacy.

"I would also like the number for the Mayor's office, please." He sounded like a snake when he said *"please"*.

Kern contained his astonishment, opened a drawer, taking a little police phone book out and paging through it. He had never called the Mayor's office before. He found the number and read it out to the priest, who spun the dial on the phone so hard I thought it would break off.

"Hello, this is Father Antonin Brown of Father Brown's Home for Boys, I would like to speak to the Mayor please." He huffed a little more to show everyone that he had made his connection. He sure had the attention of the five or so people who were standing around.

"Who is this? Vicki? Yes, I remember you, dear. Thank you for asking...the boys are doing fine...how are you doing? Two of the boys have advanced in their studies so quickly that they have been accepted to the Seminary. We're very proud of them."

Brown was making it clear that he had political as well as personal power, a definite commodity in Chicago.

"What? He's not. That's too bad, I have a particular problem." Brown was a little crestfallen, then brightened. "All right, I will speak to him."

"Mr. Deacy? Yes. Fine. Thank you. I am at your Third Area police station and the officers of the Youth Division are giving me the run-a-round about a little boy who lives at my home for boys. The child wandered away and now these people tell me that they do not have him. When I know in fact that they do have the child, and that is on the word of the Director of the Audy Home, Doctor Bagdonas, himself."

He listened for a moment. "There's a sergeant right here." He handed the phone to Kern who didn't want any part of this affair. Kern listened for a moment.

"Kern, Sergeant Joseph Kern. Yes, Sir, I am in charge. Well, the Youth Officers brought a little boy in and told the desk personnel that a priest was coming to pick the child up."

Kern looked at Brown. "And that's what happened. A priest came in and picked the kid up. Now this priest comes in here says that didn't happen....There is no run-a-round....I don't care who he is. A priest came and got the kid. It's their problem now.....Well, you do that." Kern tried to break the phone when he hung up. Now it was his turn to glare at the priest.

He turned to Flynn. "Flynn, did you or did you not see another priest come through that door and direct him upstairs to the Youth Division?" Flynn nodded, he didn't want to go on the record against this crazy priest.

Kern turned to another member of the desk staff, Bob Geraci. "Bob, didn't you tell me you saw the priest leave with a little white boy when you were locking up the gas pump?"

"Yes Sergeant. They got into a black Cadillac and pulled out of the lot. I don't know where they went from there."

Kern looked at Brown who was trying to figure out how this giant conspiracy was happening. Kern was through fooling around with it.

"Now, Fadda, first off I want to tell you that I send my kids to Cat'lic school. Every Sunday my wife takes the kids to Mass at Santa Lucia's." Kern's wife was Italian, which was why he weighed over two hundred pounds.

"And I make sure she has money to put in the basket. Every Sunday." He held up his right hand as if to swear it. Kern lived in the old neighborhood that was mostly Italians where he was affectionately known as Kraut Kern, behind his back.

Now the German Commandant came out of Kern. He wasn't an officer but he was the commander of this desk. He gave Brown his most intimidating look, which was pretty good. "Now, Fadda, you see today is Monday, and you're in my church, and I got five eye witnesses that say that a priest came in here, went upstairs and left with that boy. You can call the goddamn Pope and he ain't gonna be able to change that. One of your people has that boy, not me, so I suggest you go out and find him yourself."

"I am going to have you transferred, Sergeant…Kern!" Brown said, looking at the name plate. He didn't know when to quit.

"Good! You do that!" Kern laughed along with the rest of the desk crew. "Look around you Fadda, this is the asshole of the city. You think there's someplace worse they could send me? Ha!"

Kern turned the phone back around and put the phone book back, slamming the drawer with finality. Brown left without another comment.

Kern looked at me with one eyebrow raised. "Kelly, what the fuck are you pulling here?"

"It happened just like you said Sarge. And I'll swear to it." I winked at him.

"You're goddamn right you'll swear to it, Kelly. You put me in the middle of one of your goddamn schemes again and I'll….I'll."

"Thanks, Sarge, you're a real humanitarian." He didn't know what to think of that.

Chapter 26: The Home

Father Halloran was packing, but he wasn't looking forward to a trip to Vietnam, when Brown came storming into the facility. Everybody scattered like cockroaches. Brown called him into his office and ran down the events of the day, which sounded insane. Maybe Brown was having a breakdown, he could only hope.

"I want this Kelly to disappear! Do you understand me! And I want that boy found and returned. That ten thousand is coming out of your end." Halloran had already figured that. By his standards, he was rich and ten grand didn't mean a whole lot, other than being used as a punishment. But this *disappearing* Kelly was something beyond the call of duty, or money.

"Disappear? Father, we can't kill a policeman." Brown didn't hear a word.

"And that nurse. Well, I think we can just side line her instead. I'll call that fat faced director and have her fired."

"Father, about Kelly...uh." Halloran wanted no part of killing a cop.

"You don't have to do it yourself, delegate. There are plenty of qualified people on our list of available personnel. Don't forget how many would love to be in your position. But if you would rather go finish packing?"

There was that, although Halloran would give up his position in a heartbeat if he could. He'd thought about escaping himself, like those two kids, but he knew he could never get away from Brown. If Brown didn't just have him killed outright, he was connected around the world and had enough on Halloran to put him in prison for life. International transportation of children from a war zone for the purpose of sexual exploitation sounded like one of the charges he would be facing, for sure. He was stuck.

It was as if Brown could read his thoughts. "Relax, we can easily handle this. We're priests, the Church will cover this, just like we use these robes for everything else. We're making millions. We send sophisticated weaponry to our friends in the mercenary forces in Asia and they pay us back with ten times the value in Heroin. And we have our beautiful *Home* going here, that everyone loves so much." Brown gestured with his hand around the room and towards the big picture window that looked out on Lake Michigan.

"I could tell this Kelly was lying about the boy. He was playing cute with me. The nurse noticed my rosary and may have told him. I fear they equated the marks on the boys with the rosary." Brown almost blamed himself for whipping the boys so severely, almost, but they had deserved it after all.

"The nurse also indicated that the boy may have been sexually assaulted. That Kelly took him to the hospital for an examination. I don't know if he was examined or not, however any records mentioning sex abuse must be collected and destroyed." They shared a look.

"I disabused that Audy Home Director of the notion, but I don't think the cop or the nurse will be so easily persuaded."

Halloran knew he was in for a penny, in for a pound, now. Might as well get to work. "I'm going to need some inside help. I'd like to contact the Archdiocese and ask if we can use the services of their special investigator, Peter Sanguini. He can access those records for us."

Halloran added, "If they're hiding the boy we need to put pressure on. They're not hiding him just to be nice to the kid. They're going to use him against us." Brown agreed, they thought that everyone exploited children.

"Yes, although I think I will call the Archdiocese and speak to Cardinal Sloane personally. That way we will have his blessing if some things need to be swept under the carpet." Brown was thinking of a big carpet.

"Oh, what about the other one?" Brown asked. Halloran pointed to a cardboard box on the desk. About the size of a cigar box, it was embossed with a cross and an American flag, there was a blank space for the name of the loved one. They were used for the cremated remains of Christian military casualties of the war.

"Really," Brown picked it up, it was light.

He dismissed Halloran with a finger. To his departing back he said, "Finally did something right, tell the others that I expect penance from each one of them for this. Fifty strokes ought to be enough." Brown shook the box containing the ashes of the little drowned boy to see if it rattled, then he tossed it onto a shelf without another thought.

Chapter 27: The Curtin's

Father Michael J. Curtin was an unconventional priest and he would be the first to admit it. But Father Brown was a priest of a totally different color. Michael could hardly believe what his contacts at the Vatican had told him about Brown and his Order of Mendalin Priests. He would have to do some digging to find out more. He was just hanging up the phone, when Kelly came in the back door.

"Kelly."

"Mickey, man you saved me." Kelly gave him a big hug. Michael returned the hug warmly, Kelly was like a little brother to him and nothing was more important to him than family, nothing. A true man of God, Michael also held a unique place within the ecclesiastical rankings of the Roman Catholic Church.

"I've just been making a few calls about Father Brown and his home for boys." There was contempt in his voice. "And I saw those marks on Poc's body that you told me about."

"Poc?" Kelly looked around.

"He's up in my apartment with Ma. Making a cake." He added smiling. That sounded good.

When he wasn't in Europe, South America or trotting around the globe, Father Michael's official residence was here on Trumbull Avenue, in Chicago, the house he grew up in. Although he didn't stay here much, Ma kept it looking like he was living there full time. He mostly used it when his girlfriend was out of town. Michael had been in a relationship with an ex-nun for the last 15 years. It wasn't a big secret, but Ma pretended it wasn't happening. She didn't like his being unconventional.

When they went upstairs, Poc was icing a cake that he would probably rather have been eating. But he had enough icing on his face to tide him over until the cake was finished. He gave Kelly and Michael a genuine smile.

Ma was in her glory, fussing over the boy and hardly noticing the others in the room. She was good with kids. She had 18 grandchildren after all. They heard the door downstairs. They went down where they found Curtin in the kitchen pouring a cup of coffee from the old pot that Ma always had warming on the stove's pilot light.

"Hi, Tommy," Michael said.

"Hey, Mick. What's going on?" he said looking from Michael to Kelly, realizing that there was something going on, something bad.

Kelly said. "Sit down, man. This is going to take a while."

Chapter 28: Stephen A. Douglas Memorial

Curtin listened to Kelly with rapt attention. By the time Kelly was finished, Curtin already had a plan, the other two didn't argue, his plans were always the ones they went with anyway. Kelly's job was to call Mamma King. They were hoping she could find a more secure place for Poc. As for Michael, he was going to use his connections to find out as much as he could about Father Brown and the *Home for Boys*. Curtin decided to take the direct approach for his part of the plan.

After making a call to find out where it was, Curtin drove east on 35th Street until it ended at the foot of a pedestrian bridge that went over the Illinois Central Railroad tracks, and Lake Shore Drive, to the shore of Lake Michigan. He sat there in his car facing east.

To his left was the Stephen A. Douglas Memorial. It was an imposing marble monument towering over the entire area, topped with a bronze statue, presumably a likeness of Mr. Douglas himself.

It's not well known where Mr. Douglas is buried, it's not a busy area, but the site is a garden, kept by an old black man who lives in a little coach house on the property. The South Side of Chicago turned out to be a fitting place for a staunch abolitionist to be buried. The monument sits on property that used to be part of the Douglas Estate, which was known as *Oakenwald* in the 1800's.

On his right, to the south, Curtin looked up at a grand old yellow stone mansion. Three stories, surrounded by a tall iron picket fence that was gated in front with two huge panels that were so heavy that they had wheels on the ends to support the weight when the gates were opened or closed. They were open now during daylight, Curtin could see several vehicles parked in the rear of the facility. There was no sign that said, "Father Brown's Home for Boys."

He decided to start with the caretaker and pulled into the little parking lot of the Douglas Memorial. The old man was walking through a field of flowers with a watering can in his hand. It seemed like the flowers were caressing him as he walked. He approached Curtin, stopped a respectful distance away, put down the can and took his hat off. Curtin didn't have to say he was a policeman. The old gentleman had no doubt.

"Yes, Sa?"

"Hello. My name is Tom Curtin. What's yours?" He extended his hand. The old man was startled. He didn't answer. He looked at his own hand to see if it was dirty. It was. Curtin could not have cared less. He reached out and pumped the gentleman's hand a few times, then walked with him over to a shaded spot that had a few stone benches.

Curtin's people remembered when they were segregated and persecuted in Chicago, before Black people were even on the radar. It was less than a century ago that signs reading "*No Dogs....Or Irish*" were posted in the windows of many establishments in Chicago.

After a half hour of chatting, Curtin had a picture forming

in his head. The caretaker, Alonzo, told him that there were indeed *Chinese* boys in that old house. He said the boys were only allowed out for an hour or so, and not every day. When they were out three of the priests, the ones with the brown robes, would stand guard in a triangular pattern while the boys played soccer in the yard.

They weren't guarding against someone coming over the tall iron pickets, the old man said they were guarding against the boys trying to run away. He said he had seen it happen just last week. The ball was kicked up onto the roof of a shed. When the priests were distracted, two of the boys tried to climb over the iron fence. They were quickly snatched down by the priests and everyone went into the house. He hadn't seen hide nor hair of anyone since. There were usually about twelve boys, although Alonzo thought that they weren't always the same boys.

As they were talking Curtin saw a mail truck pull up in front of the *Home*. He had positioned himself so he could watch the building while Alonzo told him about it. He figured this was as good an opportunity to look around as any. He thanked Alonzo then beat it across the street just in time to walk up to the front door with the mail man, who was carrying two huge mail bags.

"Can I help you with one of those, partner?" Curtin asked the uniformed federal employee.

"I wish." He was struggling with the bags. "But if my supervisor saw you, I'd be fired. No civilian is allowed to handle the US mail." He said officially. Curtin shrugged, but was curious about all the orange envelopes he could see bulging out of the tops of the bags, held in only by a drawstring.

When the mail man rang the doorbell, it sounded like bells ringing to announce high mass. He just stood there and waited until the door was opened by a little man with long brown robes, bare feet. Curtin looked him over, taking note of the rosary that Kelly had told him about.

The man ignored the mail man and looked straight at Curtin. "May I help you, Sir?"

He was overly effeminate, to the point that it seemed that he didn't have a straight act. But being gay didn't mean that he was a pedophile. Curtin knew that there were gay people in the priesthood. It was a good place to be if you didn't want to have a girlfriend. No girls allowed. Seemed like a waste.

"Yes, my name is Detective Durkin from the Internal Affairs Division and I would like to see Father Brown." Curtin took his badge out of his pocket and made sure the priest got a good look. It wasn't his real one, he had several badges.

"Father Brown is in Vespers now and cannot be disturbed." That was a final answer and a dismissal, the man turned to the mail man and reached for the proffered clipboard and pen. Curtin put his arm out pushing the clipboard back into the mail man's hands.

"Well, tell him to put something on and come down here, now. I've got a missing boy on my hands and I don't have time to wait for him to finish his *toilet*." He started to push his way past the priest who held up his hands in defense.

"Oh, all right! I will get someone to help you. If you would please wait here a moment." He was in a tizzy, this is what he gets for answering the door.

"Fine," Curtin said, backing off a step. The priest signed the clipboard, turned and went back in the house, leaving the door ajar so the mail man could lug the heavy bags into the foyer.

"I've got more." The mail man said to the retreating priest who didn't respond. Then he shrugged and headed back to his truck.

Curtin, never being one to miss an opportunity, wiggled a handful of the orange envelops out of one of the bags and stuffed them into his pocket. When the mail man came back with another similarly over stuffed bag, Curtin asked how often he delivered to the home.

"Nearly every day. Not on the weekends though. But it's usually only one bag. We had a holiday last week and it throws everything off."

The little priest didn't come back. A big priest did.

Chapter 29: Cottage Grove Avenue, south bound

"Kerry....are...you...my...friend?" I was shocked, those were the first words I had ever heard from the boy. I was beginning to think that Mickey Curtin was a real miracle worker. Poc was sitting in the front seat of the car next to me. On his lap was a Tupperware container with a chocolate cake in it. In back was a little suitcase that contained a bunch of clothes Ma Curtin had materialized out of thin air.

"Of course I'm your friend Poc." What was I going to say?

"Why?" What was I going to say now?

"Why? Good question." Couldn't stall him, it would only make him suspicious of my motives. He waited for a good answer which I hoped would be forthcoming.

"Poc, you know I'm a policeman and it's my job to protect you." No comment.

"But I am also your friend and I promise that you are not going back to that place."

"You *promise*?" I almost started crying. I looked out the window for a second, it was getting dark.

"Yes, I promise. And now I'm taking you where you can

stay with some friends of mine and you will be safe." No comment.

"Uh, Poc. Was there another boy with you when you ran away?" I didn't know how to tell him. He didn't say anything, but he looked up at me, waiting.

"Well, uh, he didn't get away, Poc. He fell into the lake and he drowned."

"He still got away." Poc said, with more conviction than an 11 year old should use.

Chapter 30: The Washington's

When we arrived at the Shine King, Mamma and Allright were in the shop, Sylvester King was behind an ever growing mountain of shoes in the back, his shoe repair machines still humming. Mamma welcomed Poc with a warm hug. Allright was sort of a body guard, I figured.

"Allright going to drive you. You leave your car here, we don't want no police cars around all over the place." I didn't argue. Allright had a Plymouth Roadrunner that was a little tricked out and smelled like a case of cheap cologne had exploded inside it.

I sat with Poc in the back noticing that we were driving into what used to be the more affluent area of the South Side. We turned up Longwood Drive, a street which had a lot of hundred year old mansions that had started to be abandoned to white flight ten years ago.

There wasn't an invasion of black people, their numbers didn't increase that dramatically, just their buying power. It was the real estate brokers that peddled the panic and caused housing prices on the South Side to plummet starting in the 1950's.

Allright pulled into a circular driveway and stopped in front of a house that looked like Cyrus McCormick must have lived in it. Made of lime stone, it was three stories and had a slate roof like you would see on east coast mansions. I didn't know where the hell we were going, and Poc looked at me like he knew I was out to sea, but went along anyway. We went up the stairs and the door was opened by Mr. Cecil Washington, who was wearing a red silk smoking jacket with a velvet collar, black velvet harem pants and red slippers. He looked like a Genie. Poc and I just stared at him dumbfounded.

"Come in, Boy!" He said. "Don't be lollygagging on the porch." He probably didn't want the neighbors to see he had white visitors. It would probably lower his status in this community. Inside we were introduced to Emily, Mrs. Washington to me. She looked at that cake box and declared that some milk was needed and Poc followed her out of the room.

"Okay, I'll take care of him from now on." It was a statement and a dismissal. I couldn't let it just go at that. I had to say something stupid.

"Okay? Are you just going to keep the boy here? You can't put him in school. The people who had him aren't happy about him going missing. They're going to be looking for him." I was getting stupider by the minute.

Mr. Washington held up his hand. "I told you that the Lord pushed that boy into my arms. Don't make me tell you again." I gulped. "You got no family for him, do you? He's in my family now. My kids are grown, I've got fifteen rooms in this house and only use three or four. He can live in the rest." I was edging toward the door.

"Now you, and that trouble making brother of yours, gots to take care of them Cat'lics. That ain't my department. And as for school, my wife is a teacher. We'll let her see about that." That was as much of a dismissal as I needed, I wasn't arguing with *The Lord*. I thanked him and followed Allright out of the house after saying good-bye to Poc, who didn't seem to want to go anywhere until he finished the rest of that cake, which was going fast now that he had a gallon of milk to wash it down.

Chapter 31: The Home

"My name is Father Halloran." He was a friendly guy, but Curtin figured that was just an act. When Curtin introduced himself as Durkin, he also stuck out his hand forcing the priest to do the same. The sleeve of his robe slid back and that was when Curtin saw the tattoo on the inside of his forearm. It was a winged skull with a dagger through the right eye. He also noticed a scar in the palm of the priest's hand.

"Oh, Special Forces?" Curtin said holding the hand to look at the tattoo closer. Halloran pulled his hand away, but the smile stayed on his face, that was as far as it went though.

"Yes, we were early recon in Southeast Asia. My experiences there were what led me to the church. I met Father Brown and he opened a new way for me."

"I was in the Marines."

Curtin and Kelly were both drafted. The draft was for the Army but the Marines could take draftees if they needed them. With the war raging in Vietnam nobody was signing up for the Marines. The Army took Kelly. The Marines took Curtin. He was thrilled.

He was one of the rare few that looked forward to going to Vietnam. Only he never even made it out of boot camp. After some grueling punishment on the training quadrangle, Curtin was really starting to enjoy the tough training and was smiling. One of the Drill Sergeants slapped

Curtin and told him to wipe that smile off his face. Curtin wouldn't.

He made Curtin do a bunch of pushups and calisthenics, Curtin kept grinning. Then he started screaming in Curtin's face. When Curtin didn't back down the Sergeant challenged him to a hand to hand combat. He had bragged that he killed Viet Cong with his bare hands and with his Bowie Knife, which he wore prominently on his belt even though it wasn't part of the uniform.

They went at it tooth and nail. The Sergeant with his hand to hand deadly combat training, Curtin with his South Side street fighter training. When Curtin head butted the Sergeant and opened a gash over his eye, he started getting the upper hand. The Sergeant with his face covered in blood, pulled his big knife, taking up a stance intending to gut Curtin.

He had been pushed past the point of reason by Curtin. He had that effect on people. Curtin grinned at him, rushing the knife.

The Sergeant had started out trying to prove a point and had lost control of his emotions, Curtin had considered it a street fight from the beginning, life or death. He broke the Sergeant's forearm causing him to drop the knife, ending the fight.

His military career ended there. Curtin was given a General Discharge and escorted to the gate, not so much for breaking the Sergeant's arm, he had also bitten the guy's nose off during the fight. Apparently you bite off one nose and they hold it against you forever.

"I'm here about a missing boy. I'm with the Internal Affairs Division and I understand there's a complaint about how this boy was handled. Or maybe I should say, mishandled." Curtin had a fake smile on too, also a fake job.

Halloran stepped back into the foyer, tacitly inviting Curtin into the house. "Well, that's all cleared up now. The boy was returned and there will be no need for any *Internal* investigation."

Curtin hid his surprise. "Oh, you have the boy back, do you?"

"Yes, and he's doing well. It's such a pity that Hun drowned. You see, our boys are orphans from Vietnam and over there fishing is a way of life. The boys thought they would surprise everyone by catching some fish in the lake. Sadly they had no idea how treacherous Lake Michigan can be."

"Well, that is very sad." Curtin wasn't offering condolences. He went right on. "So, you have the other boy safe here at the Home?"

"Yes."

"Can I see him?" Curtin watched him closely.

"Of course." Halloran turned and two other priests appeared out of a doorway. They looked like they were Special Forces too. "Father Julian? Could you and Paul bring the mail in?" The two snatched up the bags like they were filled with popcorn and disappeared. Halloran asked Curtin to wait and left him alone in the hall.

The woodwork and the parquet floor wasn't just nice, it was

artwork. Where there wasn't intricate wood paneling the walls were covered in embossed leather. It looked like it had been installed yesterday, gleaming with obvious continual attention, cleaning and waxing. Curtin was running his fingers over the patterns pressed into the leather when Halloran came back with the little priest, he had a little boy in tow.

"Here we are. Poc. Say hello to the officer."

"Hello."

"I'm afraid that's about the extent of his English. We're teaching them English, but Poc is one of our new arrivals and hasn't had much study time." Halloran had his big smile back on. The little priest was behind the boy with a neutral expression on his face, one that probably scared the shit out of these kids. The boy was about 11 years old, small and thin. He looked a lot like Poc and could probably pass for Poc. Except that Curtin had already met Poc.

Curtin figured they had several other boys who could probably impersonate Poc. Didn't matter which one they used. He couldn't wait to get out of there so he thanked Halloran and the priest with no name. When he said goodbye to the boy it was like talking to a mannequin. Curtin wanted to say "*Don't worry kid. I'll be back.*"

Chapter 32: Stephan A. Douglas Memorial

When Allright and I got back to the shoe shine shop, it was closed but there was a note under my windshield wiper blade, not a note really, just a phone number. That was enough. There were no phone booths on Indiana Avenue, at least not on this part of the long street, so I went across the street to the 2nd District Station to use their phone. For free. I recognized one of the desk men and we caught up for a few minutes before I asked if I could use his phone.

I didn't actually have to ask to use the phone, I was asking to use the phone privately. He moved away and picked up some reports he had been filing. I picked up the handle and spun the dial. When the phone was answered it was a voice I had never heard before. I identified myself and waited while it sounded like the phone was being passed to another person.

"Thanks, Alonzo. Kelly?" It was Curtin. And it was late.

"Ya,"

"You got to get over here right away." This was going in the wrong direction.

"Where? What are you talking about?"

"You have to come down to the Stephen Douglas Memorial." The hell I was, this guy must be drunk.

"Are you crazy? Where the hell is the Stephen Douglas Memorial?"

"Across the street from Father Brown's Home for Boys."

"I'll be right there. What's the address?"

When I got to the end of 35th Street I saw the Memorial. The big gates were open, despite the sign that said closed at 6:00 p.m. I went right in. Curtin was in a little garden like area where he could see the building across the street to the south.

Although it was dark now there were street lights in front and flood lights around the back of the building, which I assumed was Father Brown's joint. Curtin gave me a quick rundown and asked how my day had gone. He was shocked about how Mr. Washington came into play, Curtin was afraid of him too. I couldn't believe that they had produced a new Poc. That indicated they had written the real one off. We both agreed that there couldn't be a safer place for the real Poc.

"Okay, you keep an eye on the joint. There's been a lot of traffic, cars drop people off, some driving themselves, and they had what looked like a liquor delivery a couple of hours ago. I've got to go pick up some equipment quick so we can get this surveillance going. This is a One Sixty Eight Kelly." He handed me a little pair of binoculars. I hated 168's, that's how many hours there were in a week, twenty four times seven.

I knew what *quick* meant to Curtin but this time it was ridiculous. It was 2:00 a.m., most of the cars had pulled out of their lot through the big iron gates. Some people were picked up by limos. It looked like the party was over. The only activity was a phone company truck working on a late job, a real late job, now that I thought of it.

It was Curtin, dressed in a Ma Bell Uniform complete with the truck, ladders, the whole nine yards. He pulled his truck into the Memorial lot, got out and came over to where I was dutifully watching the house. He even had a hard hat. I gave him my report. I didn't have all the plate numbers, but I did have descriptions of all the vehicles and occupants.

Although everyone was in casual clothing, we figured that they were clergy of some sort, church people for sure. A couple of the cars had placards on the rear indicating that it was a church vehicle. Priests often used them to avoid parking tickets or to prepare a traffic cop for a stop in which he would not be offered a bribe. That usually got them a pass without the cop even getting out of the squad car.

"They have six phone lines in that place." Curtin said. That was remarkable considering some people still shared a party line.

"I've got them all bugged. I'll have tapes running on all of them by tomorrow. I don't know what those priests are doing in that house, but it's more than diddling around with little boys. That priest with the tattoo on his arm looked pretty dangerous to me, and there were two more that I wouldn't want to tangle with either."

Chapter 33: Area 3 Youth Office

I didn't have to work the next day, but I stopped in to catch up on a few reports and sniff around. Actually more to see if anyone was sniffing around me. When I sat at my desk I noticed there were three notes in my typewriter roller, each indicating that Nurse Miller had called. It wasn't the number of the Audy Home but I figured that she wouldn't mind if I woke her up, even if she had worked the night shift. She answered on the second ring.

"Hello? This is Kelly." I didn't want to get into the *Officer* thing.

"Kelly. I've been fired." She didn't sound like she had been sleeping.

"Fired? Why"

"Dr. Bagdonas called me and said that I was terminated because I made false accusations against that priest. I didn't make any accusations, but if I did, they wouldn't have been false." She was fuming.

"Don't worry. I'll take care of it." I hoped.

"What can you do?"

I acted hurt, because I didn't know what I could do. "Hey, I'm doing all right so far, ain't I? If I say I'll take care of it, I will." This woman was making me nuts.

"Oh, never mind. I didn't like working there very much anyway. How is Poc?" So much for my capabilities.

"He's fine. We have him placed with a family where no one will be able to find him."

"What about the priest?"

"We're working on it. We think there are eight more boys in that Home."

"What? Oh, Kelly." She sounded like she was going to cry. I tried to distract her.

"Do you want to help?"

"Of course!"

"Good, well we're working on a plan." Curtin was, at least. "There'll be plenty of work for you when we get the rest of those kids out of there."

"You're going to get them out? How are you going to do that?"

"Well uh......the plan isn't complete yet." I had no idea.

Then, I had a great idea. "Since you don't have a job, why don't I take you to dinner tonight and I'll fill you in on what I know."

"Uh.....I don't know if I like that part of the plan."

"Come on. I'll be a perfect gentleman. Strictly business, I promise."

"Okay, if you promise."

I was making a lot of promises. None of them were easy to fulfill. She gave me her address. She lived in one of the high rise apartment buildings near Michael Reese Hospital that were mostly medical people, it was only a few blocks from the Douglas Memorial.

Chapter 34: Surveillance Van 35th Street

When I arrived for my shift Curtin had a new vehicle. It was a green phone company van parked in the alley across from the Boys Home. The inside was all tricked out with electronic equipment. I whistled.

"Where did you get all this stuff? I didn't know the Department had access to all this equipment."

"We don't. This is a loan from our friends at the F.B.I." Curtin gestured towards the tape reels that were slowly turning.

"They just gave you all this stuff?"

"They didn't want to, but I threatened to tell them what we were doing and that scared them into giving me what I wanted." I understood. Nobody wanted to play with Curtin.

"Uh, Curtin? Remember the nurse I was telling you about? The one from the Audy Home?"

"Yes." There was suspicion and a little grin on his face.

"Well, it seems that she was fired today, because of what she told me about the boy."

"Oh, that's all." Curtin didn't think much of my problem. "I'll make a call. John should be able to handle it."

John was another Curtin brother. He was the attorney turned politician of the family. He was newly elected but he was the Alderman of the 11th Ward, one of the most powerful Democratic enclaves in the country. There weren't many Republicans in Chicago. The Democrats just insulted each other before elections. John had a lot of clout now, I could only hope he could help Kay Miller.

Curtin pulled a handful of orange envelopes from his picket. They were all addressed to Father Brown's Home for Boys. He explained where he had gotten them as we began opening them.

Some of the envelopes had notes in them along with money thanking Father Brown for saving *all those boys*. As we read one note after another we gathered that Brown was telling people that he had a huge number of boys in his *Home*, Alonzo said there were ten the last time he saw them outside. There must also be brochures out there with pictures of these *poor orphans*, because those were also mentioned.

Most of the envelopes contained checks, some had cash though. Mostly dollar bills but also fives, tens and twenties. One envelope had a quarter in it with a note written in a child's hand. *Please take my milk money and buy milk for the orphans, thank you, Peter Banks.* If I had my hands around Brown's throat at that moment I would have squeezed until his damn eyes popped out.

I looked over at Curtin who was reading Peter's note over my shoulder. The look on his face was a little scary, I didn't want to know what he was thinking so I broke the tension.

"How long do I have to stay here? I've sort of got a date tonight."

Curtin grinned like the Cheshire Cat. "You don't have to stay. Allright is coming to watch the truck and tape machines. I already have some information recorded that we need to sort out."

"Allright?" I asked.

"Mamma's idea. He's getting a promotion. I'll take care of him." Then the grin was back.

"Either way you don't have a date tonight. Unless we get this worked out. Michael is meeting us at the house, he said he's got some dope on our friends across the street."

"What do you mean, no date? Do you know how long it's been since I've had a *date*?" I emphasized the word *date* to mean other things.

"No, and I don't care. You don't want a date, you want to fall in love. It's not about the *date*." He had my number.

"Whatever, I'm not missing this. And I'm not in love. I just met the girl."

"Doesn't take you long." Now I wanted to strangle him.

Chapter 35: The Curtin's Kitchen

Michael was waiting for us in the kitchen when we got to the house. Mrs. Curtin was watching Notre Dame Football in the living room. She was a diehard fan, as was everyone in the family, half of them having attended school there.

"Hi, Mike. What's up with our priest buddies?"

"Hello Jimmy. You seem to be in a hurry. Pour yourself a cup of coffee and sit."

"Oh, he met a girl and now he's in love," Curtin said to Michael.

"Again?" Michael laughed going along with the rib.

"All right, cut it out you guys. Do we have business here, or am I going to go watch the game with Ma?"

"Tommy, you hurt his feelings." Michael was digging in a little, then relented when he saw the look on my face.

"Okay, we've got a problem with *Father* Brown." There was quite a bit of doubt in Michael's voice when he said *Father*.

"More than one, I think." Curtin interjected.

"Oh? Well, the first problem then is that not only is Father Brown's orphanage and charity legitimate, he's a real priest, and so are the others in his cloister. They call themselves the Mendalin's." That was news. Curtin and I both had them pegged as fakes and con men.

He went on after making sure both of us were getting it. "Their order was started in the Netherlands, but that's legit too. And Father Brown's Home for Boys is considered one of the finest run charities and missions out there. They have a Papal Edict that gives them the right to do missionary work anywhere they want. Although it seems that they concentrate on Vietnam and the surrounding countries, they have orphanages in other countries too, including Japan, where the kids are shipped first on their way to America or one of his *Homes* in Europe. Very sophisticated organization."

"Mendalin's? What kind of Order is that?" I had never heard of it, Franciscans, Dominicans, Jesuits, those were names I expected to equate with being a priest.

"You're right Jimmy. I couldn't find anyone over here that had heard of them either. I had to call a friend at the Vatican. I found out that they're a Fundamentalist Order, obsessed with the Passion of Christ. They whip themselves with those rosaries that they wear, although they call it scourging or penance or some such crap. Some of them even inflict the Stigmata upon themselves."

My ignorance was showing on my face and he explained. "Jesus had five wounds. One in each of his hands and feet, plus the wound in his side. There have been over 300 documented cases of the miracle of the Stigmata, the first being my patron, Francis of Assisi. Their patron saint, St. Mendal reportedly received the Stigmata from God upon his death."

"What do you mean inflict it on themselves?" He had my attention now.

Michael shook his head and laughed a little, not a funny one. "These crazy bastards have themselves nailed to a cross and have a wound opened in their side. Then they hang there for a couple of hours and suffer."

"Come, on?" I wasn't going for that.

"Really Jim. There are all kinds of beliefs and traditions within the Roman Catholic Church. Why, in the Philippines during Lent people inflict suffering upon themselves that is often fatal. They think the sacrifice will cleanse their souls, insure them a seat in heaven." He shook his head again a little sorrowfully.

"And that's not all."

"Oh, goodie," Curtin said. "There's more."

Michael frowned. "This Brown character is wired in with Cardinal Sloane somehow. When I started inquiring about Brown and his *Home* to some contacts in Rome, it apparently got back here before I hung up the phone. I received a call from the Cardinal's office asking why I was interested in Brown's background. What they were really saying was, back off. I had to make something up and said I had received a donation to the Home and wanted to check it out before I passed it on."

"I'll bet they believed that, donations are what they're all about." Curtin showed Michael the envelopes and some of the contents, including Peter's letter.

"Well that explains the Papal Edict." We looked at Michael to explain what he meant by that.

"Look guys, the Catholic Church is a business. It's not God. You know some of what I do for the Church." We did. Michael, due to his calling and relationship to Elizabeth, his sister that married into the Mafia, was the bagman for the Vatican.

He had been chosen to travel around the country, and the world, collecting donations from organizations and individuals that, although they were criminal entities, still wanted to hedge their bets and send some insurance money to the Church.

Michael didn't have a parish or a congregation but he was one of the most important men in the Catholic Church just by reason of everything he knew. Knowing he didn't need to explain what he did for the Church, he continued speaking.

"There are many ways to get a Papal Edict, which is a license to collect money basically. The best way to receive an Edict is to send a big '*deposit*' to the Director of the Vatican Bank. The Director is Cardinal Renzini, that guy would prostitute his mother for a lira." He looked at Curtin. "So what do you figure their take is considering how many of these envelopes you saw?"

"They could probably clear at least four, five thousand on each bag and they get five or six bags a week. They must have a vast network to distribute and collect these donation envelopes. Brochures, school drives, backed by corporate sponsors who get huge tax breaks. Very professional. Considering they're branching out into narcotics and weapons dealing, they are raking in millions." Curtin had a calculator for a brain although this was the first I was hearing about narcotics and weapons.

"With that kind of money to buy influence, no wonder nobody has a bad word to say about them." I said.

"I've got plenty of bad words for them. I can't believe they're priests, the things they do and the way they talk about it." Curtin had the floor now. "I listened to a lot of their phone calls, local and international. I made a call myself to a guy I know who's in the C.I.A. They raise money supposedly to save orphans and to send farm equipment and supplies to war ravaged people in South East Asia, but what they're actually sending is our latest weapons technology. They also have a pipeline to smuggle heroin back here somehow. The only *orphans* that they're *saving* are the ones that they hand pick for their sex trafficking business."

Michael and I both whistled, it was making sense now. "Incredible. And the South Side is the perfect place to distribute the narcotics and still have a cover."

Curtin wasn't done yet. "That Boy's Home is unique to the United States I think, but places like that are common in other countries, especially in Thailand and some in Europe, like in Amsterdam. They're basically brothels for child sexual predators."

"Some of the things that they want those children to do would turn your stomach. And they act like they're ordering dinner. In fact dinner and drinks are part of the package, afterward you take your kid upstairs and have your fun. And they're booked up until New Year's."

"There has to be extensive records in that house. They have the potential to blackmail anyone who uses the facility but the first thing we have to do is get those boys out of that house. If you saw the look on the face of that boy that they said was Poc...."

Curtin gave his brother a look that had finality in it. "Michael, I don't care if they're priests. They could all be Cardinals, it doesn't matter, there has to be...." He bit it off. I glanced at Michael, neither of us wanted to know what he was planning.

Michael stood up, came around the table and placed his hands on top of our heads. He began to pray. I couldn't understand the language but the intent was clear. I understood the word *absolve*, but didn't understand what I was being forgiven for, maybe it was for what I was going to do. When he was finished, he switched back to English.

"Father Dolan at Nativity of Christ will open the church early for me to say mass tomorrow. Eight o'clock, and bring Ma." He added to Curtin. It wasn't a request. I doubted my date would last all night anyway. I had church in the morning now too.

Chapter 36: Chinatown

"This is a terrible idea." Kay kept telling herself that as she rode the elevator down. When Kelly rang her bell, she had jumped even though she was expecting him. Then instead of inviting him up to her apartment, she said she would meet him in the lobby. This was a terrible idea. Cops were just one step above of doctors on her eligibility list. Doctors being on the bottom. She hated doctors, arrogant bastards, surgeons were the worst. God's gifts to the world. She hadn't dated enough cops to hate them all. Maybe this one would tip the scales. One positive sign at least, Kelly had a car. She firmly believed the last guy she dated only asked her out because she had a car.

He was waiting for her in the lobby with that silly Irish grin on his face. He seemed to read her thoughts and lost the grin. That was a little better. He had brown curly hair that seemed to have a mind of its own. She smiled and tried to be nice, after all he was paying for dinner, she hoped. She'd dated a couple of *Dutchmen* too.

"Hi. You look great." When he said it, she couldn't even remember what she was wearing and had to glance down at herself before she said *thank-you.*

He noticed and just stood there. "I'm sorry, Jim. I'm worried about Poc. And thinking about where I'm going to go apply for a job." She figured if she called him by his first name it might deflect from the mood she was emanating, and it did.

"Oh, don't worry. Come on. Let's go get something to eat

and I'll fill you in. Do you like Chinese food?" She hated chop suey, but said she loved Chinese food anyway. Chicago's Chinatown was not as big as San Francisco's certainly. It was only a few blocks long surrounded by a neighborhood that had just as many Italians as Chinese, but it had a unique international feeling and charm.

By the time two hours had flown by, she had changed her mind about Chinese food and cops, well maybe one cop. The food was exotic, not chop suey, dumplings, and salt and pepper shrimp, and delicate soups with crisp vegetables. For the main course, he ordered a steamed pike, which was decorated like a work of art when it arrived on a huge plate. That was her favorite. Actually everything was her favorite. She asked him how he had found this unique place on Wentworth Avenue, where every doorway was a different Oriental restaurant.

"Two things Irishmen know," he said. "Where to find good whiskey and good Chinese food." She found herself laughing easily with this curious man. He asked her questions about herself, saying 'I *knew it*' when she told him she had been a captain in the Army Medical Corps.

Kelly told her about his experience in the Army and how he was blown up by a cook stove. It sounded very familiar, but she didn't want to ask him when and where it had taken place, deciding to ask a friend of hers to look it up later. When she asked about Poc, he hesitated. The news about Poc was encouraging and distressing at the same time.

"Well, can I go see him?"

"Not right away, I think we should see how this is going to

develop. I'm sure we're going to need your services when we get the rest of the boys out of there."

"Oh, Kelly. I'm so happy, you're going to get them out. I can help, I'll do anything you want!" She blushed when she realized the double meaning of what she had said. Kelly acted as though he didn't catch it.

"I think that Father Brown is a seriously dangerous character," he said, trying to cover her embarrassment.

"You're telling me. Those eyes of his. They're grey like his hair. Scary. If you told me he was the Devil himself, I wouldn't doubt you for a second." She shivered thinking about him holding her hand.

The last course of the dinner was a steaming pot of oolong tea and two fortune cookies. It was brought to their table by their waiter who wore a starched white jacket and was apparently a friend of Kelly's.

Kelly broke his cookie and read the fortune out loud, laughing, "*You will soon receive spiritual enlightenment.*" After glancing at her own fortune she quickly said she didn't believe in fortunes and changed the subject.

Kelly took her home, didn't ask to be invited upstairs, kissed her lightly on the cheek and left saying that he had church in the morning. Church in the morning? First time she had heard that one.

She didn't know what to think about Kelly and the entire situation. The things that were happening were hard to believe. She had said she didn't believe in fortune cookie fortunes because she didn't want Kelly to see hers. She had

it in her hand now as the elevator went to the tenth floor.
She looked at it again.......

Chapter 37: Nativity of Our Lord Church

The pretty little church on 37th Street was familiar to all those who were attending Michael's mass. There was: Mrs. Curtin, all dressed up like it was Easter Sunday; Patrick, the contractor, his wife and five children. The Chicago Fireman, Daniel, his wife and four children; and John, the Alderman, with only three kids and his beautiful politician's wife. Curtin's sister, Liz, was there with her clan: her six children and Nicky Fellino, her husband. Even though Nicky was one of the top guys in what passed for the Chicago Mafia, he was second banana in his family. And he didn't seem to mind that his wife ran the family. She had given him five boys and a beautiful girl, just like her mother. And then of course there was Curtin and me, the two disappointments, with no wives no kids.

Two of Elizabeth's sons were the altar boys. The rest of us all packed into the front pews and enjoyed Michael's mass. I loved going to his masses. Michael had a way of making you feel as though you were there with Jesus, participating in the Last Supper. At the end, he blessed each one of the children in turn, having lined them up in a chorus line. They were thrilled. All the kids loved Uncle Mike. The adults did too.

Afterwards we went to a little restaurant where they pushed together a couple of tables so the kids and wives were isolated and the damage could be contained somewhat. The men all settled at another table and Curtin proceeded to tell the guys about Father Brown's Home for Boys, halting when the waitresses came to fuss over us. This was always a big check and a big tip for them.

Patrick had an Irish temper, short. "I say we just go there, bust the door down and take those kids. And if any of those perverts tries to stop us, all the more fun." He made a fist that was as big as a cabbage. Good thing Pat wasn't the one who made the plans!

Curtin calmed him down as best he could explaining that there was more to it than just the kids. "We can take those kids out of there any time we want, sure. But then they will just ship in another load of boys and start the same shit in another location." There were nods around the table.

"Plus they have other businesses that we need to include in any planning. They have a big warehouse on Halsted. I haven't had a chance to check the place out yet."

"Where on Halsted? That is my territory." Nicky was automatically a participant in any family business and he was a valuable ally. He knew he could tell us anything. We were family first, and cops later at this table.

"4253 South Halsted." Curtin answered, then added. "Nick, I could use a couple of guys for a few days. Could you help us out?"

"For this, I will give you an army. And I will find out what's going on over on Halsted." He glanced over at his boys who were throwing food at each other, while being scolded by everyone else, and smiled.

When Nicky mentioned territory, it reminded me of the

Policy Runners and their territories. I asked him if he knew anything about Policy on the South Side.

"Sure, but we let the Melenzana have that business. It's too penny-ante for us. Now, if they want to get into other things, they have to ask first and then we get a cut." Very business-like, for crime.

"How about heroin?" I said. Curtin looked at me and I could see the light go on. The priests had to have a way to distribute their drugs. They sure weren't going to stand on the street corner and deal heroin balloons in priest robes.

"Now that's not penny-ante. Do you have something else that we need to discuss other than these *farabutto* priests?" I didn't know what he said in Italian, but Michael made the sign of the cross.

"I don't know, yet. It may be all connected. I just wanted to know whose toes I would be stepping on if I started looking into what the Policy people are doing.

"Momma Donna! Fratello Mio, you do whatever you want! I'll take care of the Melenzana. But you know, they must be putting some money in someone's pocket?" He meant paying off Vice cops. Curtin looked at me. We knew what he meant.

Chapter38: Area 3 Youth Office

Monday morning, bright and early, I arrived at my desk to find someone already sitting behind it, in my chair. He looked like a Homicide Detective, all decked out in a three piece silk suit, starched shirt and colorful tie, but even better than our dicks. I could tell this guy had his clothes made by the best tailors money could buy. His hair was longish and greasy, but he was definitely a high roller. Gold Cartier watch, a lot of other showy jewelry to impress people, a typical fixer if I had to guess.

He stood up when I stopped in front of my desk.

"Kelly?" He stuck out his hand. Calcaterra and Frankie Bartuca were on the other side of the squad room, acting disinterested, but watching closely. He must have come in and asked for me and then made himself at home, at my desk. They knew that would piss me off. They were enjoying this.

I shook his hand. "What can I do for you?" I didn't give a shit what his name was. All I wanted was my desk back.

He came around and sat on the edge of my desk, trying to be casual. Looking up at me a little, "My name is Pete Sanguini. I used to be with the Department, Area 6 Homicide. Now I work for the Archdiocese of Chicago as a Special Investigator." He pulled a card out of his vest pocket and handed it to me.

"I said, what can I do for you?" I just looked at him unimpressed, until he became uncomfortable enough to get his ass off my desk.

I looked down at the card, which probably cost the Church a buck each. His name was in gold with his title underneath it, the card had a Miter and crossed religious symbols on the left side, three colors, embossed with gold leaf that I didn't doubt was 24 karat.

"All right. If that's how you want to play it. What you can do for me is give me that Vietnamese boy." I looked over to see if Calcaterra and Frankie were listening too, but they were too far away to hear what he said. I shouldn't have done even that though, as Sanguini noticed and pressed his point.

"We know you have the kid, Kelly." He was matter of fact about it. I hoped the whole thing wasn't unraveling. I would have to contact Mamma and Mr. Washington, tell them to be careful. I stayed still, not even changing my expression.

"Look, Kelly, this could be the thing that makes you." He was getting friendly now. "What's your wildest dream? Promotion? Money? All you have to do is give Brown the kid and forget everything you've done or heard about the matter."

I couldn't contain myself. "Everything? Do you know anything about Father Brown?"

This guy was way ahead of me. "I know everything about everything. I know that nurse told you the kid was molested and you took the kid to the County, although there's no record of it. What I can't figure out is why you give a shit, and neither can my...uh...superiors. That's why they asked me to approach you and smooth this whole thing over before it becomes a problem."

He smiled like a pirate, moved in a little closer, conspiratorially speaking. We were confidants now. "I handle *all* the sex complaints that are made against the Archdiocese. Easier than homicide and the pay is much better."

He chuckled, giving me the buddy grin on that one. "These *supposed* victims are usually all perverts that just want to try and get settlement money from the Church. I start digging up the dirt on them the minute they make the complaint. Nine out of ten times I find enough dirt to make them drop the whole thing or settle for a few bucks." He chuckled again, very proud of himself. If snakes could laugh that is what they would sound like.

He was being frank with me, now it was time to hear the threats. "So what's it going to be, Kelly? They can hurt you as well as help you. They were going to have you fired, but I told them to hold off for now, until I talked to you. You know, one cop to another.

Apparently that was all the threatening he thought he needed. Back to the one copper to another talk. "Now you want be a Sergeant, boom you're Sergeant Kelly. Money? Name your price. You can have whatever you want. All you have to do is produce the kid, see?"

He crossed his arms, smiling at me as he sat back down on the edge of my desk, quite pleased with his proposal. He was finished. So was I. If I understood him right this

Sanguini's job was to discredit the legitimate complaints of people who were sexually abused by clergy. To make the victims seem to be the guilty ones instead of the priests. Then to threaten them with this information so they would settle or withdraw their accusations.

"So, you want to know if I see you?" I looked at him expressionless.

"Yea." He was a cocky now, thinking he had me. He had no idea!

"Okay, I'll see you....and I'll raise you five." I hauled off and slapped him in the side of his head as hard as I could. If my hand had come off, it wouldn't have been hard enough. To his credit, he didn't go all the way down, but I managed to knock him off my desk.

When he jumped up and moved toward me I already had my snub nose in my hand. I motioned towards the door with the barrel. "You can give 'Them' that answer. Now move it."

I thought he was going to go for it and opt for the pistol whipping I was dying to administer, but he thought better of his impulse looking down the barrel of my snub nose. He fingered his hair back into place, straightened his jacket and turned towards the door.

Before he moved, I said, "Oh, and if 'They' do manage to get me fired, you can expect another raise," and I pointed upward with the barrel of my gun. He got the message.

As he was leaving, Calcaterra and Bartuca couldn't contain themselves any longer and horse laughed him out the door for good measure. I wasn't laughing, although I was certain it couldn't have made matters worse for me if I did. I called Curtin.

Chapter 39: Area 3 Youth Commander's Office

"Good! I love it when you get violent, Kelly." He was laughing like an idiot. A true Stooge, Curtin liked anything where people got slapped in the head.

"Come on. I never should have lost my temper. Now, I've got to be looking over my shoulder for that grease ball from now on."

"Well, there is that." I hated it when he was obvious.

"What should I do?"

"Just wait, it will come to you." Several hours later it did.

I was thinking about taking a ride and going to look for Franklin Palmer and his Policy dealing mother when the phone rang in the lieutenant's office and he came out and gave me the finger, the crook one.

Lt. Wojohowski was old school. We had an unsaid agreement: I did my work and he left me alone. "It's your father." He said to me by way of warning. "You can use my office."

I thanked him like the condemned prisoner thanks the hangman so he doesn't screw up, leaving you dangling and strangling.

Before I picked up the phone, I let all of the emotions run through me and tried to get focused. "Hello."

"What the hell are you doing? I thought the Youth Division would keep you out of trouble. The Cardinal, the fucking Cardinal! asked the Mayor to fire you because you're spreading salacious lies about one of the most pious priests in the whole goddamn Roman Catholic Church! For Christ's sake!"

"Nice to hear your voice, Dad."

"Don't get cute with me, James. I just had to put my job on the line to save your ass, *again.*"

As long as a certain highly placed political official was alive, my father was incapable of losing his job. My father, James W. Kelly, Senior, was a Captain with the Chicago Police Department. He was promoted to this lofty position not for his competence, rather for the reason that he had gotten every other promotion since he was a motorcycle cop and was run over by a drunken alderman during the Bud Billiken Day Parade.

That alderman moved up in the world and so did my father. Now, he was one of the top cops in the patrol division, and that was probably as high as he would get, because it was well known that he was an alcoholic. They couldn't give him a position, where they couldn't watch him.

"Thank you. So what are the conditions under which I received this favor?" I knew there would be stipulations.

"Nothing." I was surprised, or they weren't telling him anything. "Just leave anything that has to do with the Church alone. That's all." He was calming down, I could tell he had been drinking and I knew how to ride the waves.

"That's what I'll do then. Don't worry, Dad. I won't bother them, in fact I'm looking for a black kid right now that's wanted for murder and he…"

"Good. Good. A black kid wanted for murder. Concentrate on that." He said, and hung up.

My father and I had a strange relationship. I knew he loved me, but I represented too much pain for him to think about me. There wasn't enough booze in the world to make him forget about the day my mother and sister were both killed when they were broadsided in an intersection where my mother had not stopped for a stop sign. It was on Christmas Eve. I wasn't in the car but I was the only survivor. You learned to live with it or it slowly killed you, like it was killing him.

Chapter 40: Surveillance Van 35th Street

Curtin had spent the day listening to tapes, plus he was correlating information that was coming in from his other sources at the same time. That would have been confusing enough but he was really worried about Kelly's run in with the Archdiocese investigator, Sanguini.

The resulting call from his father, *Captain Kelly*, was also interesting. It indicated these people had real power. Kelly was lucky his old man had a heavy clout, in Chicago it was power against power all the time. Being preoccupied he almost missed it when someone mentioned Kelly's name on the tape. He wound the reel back a bit.

"That's right. James Kelly. You have his address, the vehicle he drives, even a picture of him, what more do you need? Just go there and kill him and then take the body over and have Goddard dispose of it."

"When?"

"Now, tonight, you idiot. Sanguini blew it, so now we're cleaning everything up and sweeping it under the Cardinal's rug."

"Whose?"

"Never mind, that's not for you two to worry about. We're covered. That's all that matters. Do you have the proper weapons for this assignment?"

"Yes, Father. With noise suppressors."

"Report back to me when you've accomplished your mission, Brother."

Kelly got there for his shift just then, Curtin played the tape for him.

"Didn't take long to move from having me fired to making me dead, did it?" Kelly was trying to make a joke and failing.

"All the same, you better not go home tonight. You can stay up in Michael's apartment, his girlfriend is back so he won't be up there."

Kelly wasn't very happy about this latest development. He was looking at the list that Curtin had been compiling when he recognized a name, Johnny Slater.

"Curtin, how'd you come across this name?"

"I think he's one of the contacts to the drug distribution. Why?"

"His name came up in another case I've been working on. He was the first one accused of murdering a girl that lived downstairs from the Policy woman, whose son confessed to the murder. Slater was supposedly just the girl's pimp, but now I think he may have bigger aspirations."

Curtin, who had been listening to Kelly with a head set speaker up to one ear, suddenly threw down the head set and started pulling plugs.

"Come on. They're wise to us!" He exclaimed. Kelly started following Curtin's lead, turning off the tape machines and pulling the plugs that ran through a port in the side of the van. Curtin was peeking through a curtain that hid the rear of the van from prying eyes. He cursed. Jumping into the front seat he rip started the van and drove down the alley leaving the wires dangling from the telephone box up on the pole.

Chapter 41: Kelly's House

While Mrs. Curtin was fussing over Kelly, demanding he choose from a number of pillows she was offering, Curtin said he had to go out for something and left them. He went down to the basement first to pick up a few items that he might need, then he headed for Kelly's house. Kelly lived in the basement of a bungalow that wasn't supposed to have an apartment in the basement, which is why it was so cheap.

The landlord and his wife were Bohemian and lived upstairs, which is the reverse of the old Bohemian joke he remembered from childhood. *'Why don't Bohemians get hurt if their house catches fire....because you can't get hurt jumping out of a basement window'*. Curtin didn't get the point of the joke but one thing he did know about the house with the apartment in the basement was that someone was coming there to kill Kelly and possibly the kindly Bohemian landlord and his wife too.

It was a quiet residential street, but the house was on the corner of a busier street and that's where the two guys who came for Kelly parked to stalk their prey under the cover of the heavy traffic on 47th Street. Curtin took his time waiting to see if they were smart enough to back their play and when he saw that they were alone he went looking for something to make an impression on them.

There was a City of Chicago maintenance yard under the famous overpass that had been built to ease traffic on Ashland Avenue. Curtin opened a pad lock with a pick and pushed the gate wide. Once in the yard he went over to one of the big salt trucks that they were prepping for the upcoming season. Chicago had two seasons, the green season and the white season. They had already put the snow plow on the front of the truck, although there was no salt in it. The salt was being piled up in a huge mountain at the back of the yard, waiting for the first snow, which was hopefully months away.

Hoping that the truck he chose had been gassed up, Curtin took only a few seconds to hot wire the ignition, crank it over and rev up the powerful engine. He pulled out of the lot without anyone even noticing a snow plow moving out to plow streets that had no snow.

Curtin cruised along towards Kelly's house, going slowly through the gears, stopping at lights, starting without too much jerkiness. When he was close he could see the car he was looking for still parked in the same spot, shame these guys were real amateurs, he downshifted in order to pick up speed. The huge plow on the front of the truck was bouncing up and down because there wasn't the weight of the salt to counter balance it, but Curtin didn't care he just kept building speed, holding the gas pedal to the floor.

The two guys that had come to kill Kelly didn't know what was happening until it was way too late, which was the plan. When Curtin crashed the plow into the front of their car, head on, full speed, he laughed at the expression on their faces just before impact. The truck pushed their car about twenty feet before Curtin hit his air brakes and stopped both vehicles. The plow was nearly up to the windshield of the car.

Curtin jumped out of the truck, looking around to see if there were any *pain in the ass* bystanders in sight. Seeing no one, he went over to the passenger side of the demolished vehicle, leaned into the window as if to try and help these two unfortunate men. He saw their long barreled silenced weapons on the floor.

They were both out of it, a lot of blood and head trauma, most probably dead already. Curtin pulled something out of his pocket, pulled a pin on the device and dropped it on the floor of the car. He reached in, taking a wallet out of the passenger's pocket, putting it in his own pocket. He looked around once more for witnesses. Seeing none, he just strolled away.

He was about half a block down the side street when he heard a muffled poof, there was a flash of light behind him and the shadows of flickering flames. There was no need to turn around to see the car burning. He heard screaming, that certain kind of high pitched screaming you would expect to hear when someone was being burned alive. He'd guessed wrong. They were still alive. If you planned to kill people, you should also plan on the possibility of them killing you first. He kept walking.

Chapter 42: Area 3 Youth Office

"ALL UNITS. ALL UNITS. Be on the lookout for a kidnapped newborn infant. Just taken from Cook County Hospital approximately one hour ago. The baby is a male black 6 pounds 9 ounces 20 inches long. The offender is possibly a female, black, medium build wearing a white nurse's uniform, white shoes and cap." I had just started up the squad in the Area lot, when the call came out. Shutting the ignition of the car off, I headed back upstairs knowing they would just call me back in if I went anywhere.

I had been confused this morning when Curtin told me that I could go back home whenever I wanted, but when I went home to change, and saw the burned out vehicle with the snow plow all smashed together across the street, I was pretty sure that he had something to do with it.

By the time I reached the Youth Office, it was bedlam. Wojohowski was yelling at Toolis which he never did.

"It's our job! That's what downtown said."

"But Kidnapping is a Homicide Division crime. It's in the book."

"What book? There's no fucking book. I'll tell you what's in the book, the Deputy called me and said it was our assignment. That's in the book. And you can take that to the bank. We may have to, if we don't find that kid. We may end up being bank guards!"

"Speak of finding lost kids, here's our expert lost kid finder now." Toolis was using me to deflect from the Lieutenant's hysteria. Shit flows downhill.

"You got any expert ideas as to where this kid might be, Kelly"

"Not really Sarge, not where he is, no." Toolis huffed and turned back to the Lieutenant as if to show he wasn't the only person who was clueless.

"But I think I may have seen the kidnapper."

"WHAT!" There were six people in the squad room and they all said it at the same time, like a chorus.

Now I had twelve eye balls boring into me. "Well, I'm not sure." There were a couple of 'I *told you so comments.*' "But ya see, I was at the County Hospital waiting in the hall, and um, I saw a pregnant woman who didn't act like she was pregnant."

"You're a genius Kelly! You solved it! That is the smoking gun right there," Frankie mocked.

"Enough." Wojo said, silencing the crowd. "What did you see, Kelly?"

I cleared my throat. "I saw a woman with a big belly get hit with a door, right in the stomach, and she didn't even flinch." I was buttering it up a little. There was no applause.

"She was standing outside the Maternity Clinic door, looking in." Not even an interested nod from anyone, *Skeptics* was the first class taught on the street. "Really, the nurse who hit her with the door was more freaked out than the pregnant woman was."

"Well, that sounds like a promising lead, you work on it yourself for now, Kelly," the Lieutenant said, meaning *'that was the stupidest thing I've ever heard.'* Everybody went back to what they were doing, my idea was so lame they didn't even bother to kid me about it anymore.

I didn't say anything about seeing her getting on the bus. No one thought I had a shot anyway, that was no more proof of anything. But I did remember the bus number. 22A Indiana Ave., was the bus that Curtin and I always took to and from the gym where we trained for the Golden Gloves when we were kids. It stopped at the hospital, I remember, because we were always afraid we would catch a disease from anyone who got on at that stop.

So I went to the Hospital and sat on the bench at the bus stop. There were police, TV news and official vehicles parked everywhere. People were running in and out of the hospital, even Wojohowski and Toolis who never left the office showed up, but no one paid any attention to me.

Chapter 43: The Home

"Burned?" Brown couldn't believe what he was hearing. "How did they get burned?"

"Well, the police say that some kids must have stolen the truck and crashed it into them. Then it caught fire. But I don't believe it." Halloran was always suspicious. It kept him alive.

"What do you believe?"

"I told you that telephone van was across the street for several days."

"Right, and when I went to look, it had mysteriously disappeared." Brown was skeptical of everything as a rule, he thought it kept him in a superior position.

"I think it disappeared, because they were listening to our phone calls and they got spooked. You were on the phone when I mentioned the van in the alley. How else did they know that I had sent that team over to Kelly's house? That was no coincidence."

"Taping our phones?" If true this was very bad, Father Brown thought, he had been conducting a lot of business on the phone.

"What do you think we should do?" There it was. Halloran finally being asked what they needed to do.

"I think we should shut down this operation, move the boys and see what the opposition does next."

"What opposition? Kelly? He's no opposition."

"Kelly didn't kill those two in the car last night, and he couldn't have set up that monitoring van without professional help. Federal help."

"We do have a Federal contract, and we can't afford to lose that," Brown mused, as he sat in his leather chair behind the antique mahogany desk. Finally, he came to a decision, the same one that Halloran had already suggested.

"The boys will have to be moved. The...uh...extra-curricular activities will have to be postponed." He pounded his fist on the desk bouncing everything on top despite the weight of the mahogany.

"I want all these people dead! Dead! Do you hear? I don't care if they're federal or local. Get as many people as you need. And get a hold of Slater and that other one with the big hair. Tell them that there will be changes. Damn it! God curse them all!"

Halloran knew Brown would be scourging himself over this outburst. He shrugged his shoulders a little and could feel the fifty lashes he had given himself with the rosary, at Brown's orders. He thought fifty for Brown would be a good start.

"Well, get going! Get Francis and get those kids ready to move," Brown shouted.

"Move them where, Father?" Halloran was through offering suggestions.

Brown's eyebrows went up with an idea. "Take them to the

facility on Halsted. Set them up with cots in the conference room on the second floor. We can move the mail in there and they can start processing it there. And if they become a liability they're already in a place where we can easily dispose of them."

"Dispose of them? Father?" Halloran was a little shocked at the callousness of the priest. He had killed many people in the name of God and country but eight little boys, some of whom he had a peculiar affection for?

"Do you want them to be interviewed by authorities?" There was that. "Besides they're animals. Buddhists, no matter how hard we try to convert them. The world would be better off with a few million less of those heathens. Nobody's going to miss eight.

Chapter 44: Curtin's Basement Lab

Curtin and Michael were down in the basement, in Curtin's workshop. It looked like a cross between a bomb factory and Dr. Frankenstein's laboratory. They were sitting at a long heavy work bench that Curtin had gotten from a woodshop classroom at a Catholic School that was closed due to white flight. The new people that were moving into those neighborhoods were Baptists. Not only did property values suffer, but local communities were torn apart by crooked real estate agents.

"I wanted you to listen to this, tell me what you think." Michael figured his brother already had a good idea of what was on the tape and was looking for confirmation. Curtin clicked the switch and the reels started turning. A voice came out of the little cloth covered speaker, a voice that Michael knew very well.

"Please.......Please......Antonin! I need you. I need it now." The voice was wailing, choking with tears.

"I told you no. I asked you for help and you failed."

"I didn't fail, he did." The voice snorted back tears. "You know I would do anything for you. Just ask. But please, please I need to come there now. I need contrition." He pleaded.

"No. I told you the boys are too busy working. With the one that your man couldn't find still out there, I don't feel that having anyone come here would be wise."

"I *am not anyone!*"

"*Yes, your Eminence.*" There was heavy sarcasm in his voice. "*I know who you are, but that doesn't change anything.*"

Curtin clicked off the tape. He looked at his brother, who was visibly shaken. There was no need to ask him if he had just heard the voice of Cardinal Sloane. "He's apparently one of their biggest customer's. Brown treats him like a dog. Makes him beg and then refuses him. It sounds like the Cardinal goes there at least once a week, has a few drinks, blesses the boys then honors one of them with rape. After that, Brown comes in with that rosary he wears and whips the shit out of Sloane for good measure. That part I like."

"Dear God." Michael sighed.

"Not in that house, Mick. I've got people watching the place. In just a few days we've recorded seventeen priests using their *facility.* Plus dozens more making reservations on the phone. It's a big business for Brown, his *penitents,* as he calls them, shell out thousands for his unique services. It's also a cash only business. And of course they're all potential blackmail victims should any of them reach positions of authority, like the Cardinal."

Michael came out of his shock a little bit. "If Brown has placed the Cardinal is such a compromising position I don't see how we can do anything within the Church structure here. The Vatican wouldn't believe that tape, they would refer any official complaints to the Cardinal's office regardless of anything we say or could even prove about Brown's activities. I'm going to have to work on that. Sloane, although apparently an extremely sick individual, is the supreme word on anything within the Chicago Archdiocese."

The extension phone Curtin had installed in the basement rang along with the one upstairs and he picked it up right away, listening to a short message. "Okay Alonzo, thanks."

"Shit! I've got to go. They're moving the kids."

Chapter 45: Cook County Hospital

"Do you remember a pregnant woman getting on the bus here on Tuesday around seven o'clock?" I was surprised by how many busses were on this one route. I had been talking to one driver after another for about three hours and hadn't seen the same one twice, however, the route was miles long going to the end of Indiana Avenue. I wondered how many drivers there were. I'd had no luck so far.

"Man that's all that rides this bus to and from this hospital is pregnant women." Considering the last three hours I'd spent sitting on the bench at the bus stop, I knew he was right. I reframed the question.

"This one was different. You know how when a woman is real pregnant they have trouble walking and especially climbing steps because the baby is low?" He thought about it for a moment. The windows were all open and the fumes from the diesel engine were hanging heavier in the air the longer we sat there but it had been my idea, and it was looking like a bad idea. The fumes didn't seem to bother him much.

"Yes." That was all he said, this wasn't going anywhere.

"Well, did you notice a woman who was real pregnant get on your bus and hop right up the stairs like she wasn't even pregnant?"

"Yes." He said. Jackpot! I wanted to kiss him.

"But she ain't pregnant no more." He added.

"What are you talking about?" One moment up and the next down.

"Why she had that baby man. She showed it to me this morning when she got on the bus during my first run. Cute little boy."

"Holy Shit!" I couldn't believe it. Was it the kidnapped baby?

"Do you know where she got off the bus?" The million dollar question.

"Yea man, she been on my bus before. She gets off at 47th Street." Going back up. That meant she lived within walking distance of 47th and Indiana. It was a big city but the part that I needed to search had just gotten a lot smaller.

"But she gets a transfer too." Crash and burn, she transferred to another bus at 47th Street. She could go east or west from Indiana, half of the South Side of the city to search. My search area had just gotten a lot bigger.

Chapter 46: Area 3 Youth Office

I tried a few drivers on the 47th Street bus route, but didn't have any luck. Finally, I gave up when it was getting toward the end of my shift. When I got back to the area the unit was empty. Everybody must have been out beating the bushes for the missing baby. There were a number of notes, on scrap paper, rolled under my typewriter bar.

One was from Kay Miller marked *very important* and one with Curtin's name and a phone number, no further information. Curtin's didn't leave any details but I knew Kay's *very important* couldn't beat Curtin's number. It was the phone at the Douglas Memorial coach house. I called Curtin.

"Kelly, I'm glad you called. They moved the kids."

This was a disaster. "They're gone, everybody?"

"No just the kids, but there's no partying going on either. I think we spooked them with the telephone van."

"Well, do we know where the kids are?"

"No, Allright was watching the Home when a van pulled up and the priests started bringing the kids out. He ran over here real quick to call me, but the priests were faster. They loaded the boys up and took off. Allright tried to catch up with them, but lost them west bound on 35th Street somewhere. Kid feels real bad."

"Sure, not his fault. How are we going to find out where they took the boys?"

"I think we may try it Patrick's way. We need someone to talk to."

"Oh, no. Not Patrick's way."

"These people are pissing me off." That was bad for them, very bad.

"What else have you found out?" I knew he had something.

"That warehouse on Halsted is a government installation. It's part of the Army's Graves Registration Division. Nicky Fellino called me and said that he has a contact who said that they go to Midway Airport in army trucks once a week and pick up sealed coffins coming in from Hawaii. In these coffins are the bodies of soldiers killed in Vietnam, who have not been claimed. No family, unable to be identified, cases like that. I can't figure out what they have to do with Father Brown."

And that was the thing that was pissing him off.

"So what's the plan, rubber band?" It didn't rhyme but it was something we had said to each other in cases like this since we were kids. Curtin had a plan of course.

"Can you get your girlfriend...?"

"She's not my girlfriend."

"Whatever, can you get her to go and check out the kids when we spring them from where ever they are and get them someplace safe?"

"I can do better than that. I've got a Vietnamese doctor who I'm sure would be happy to treat the boys. All I've got to do is get Kay to get him set up for when we have the kids, which will be when?"

"One thing at a time. Right now you're on stand-by. You talk to *Kay* and get that doctor and just be ready. I'll find out where they're keeping the boys. Then we just go get them, no problem." I hated it when he said 'no *problem*'. There obviously was a problem.

"No problem? What's the problem, Curtin?" I knew this guy.

"I think they're planning on harming those boys."

Chapter 47: Meadow Lakes Apartments

When her phone rang Kay Miller picked it up while it was ringing.

"Kelly?" She had been praying for it to ring, waiting. When she heard Kelly's voice, she was immediately relieved and angry with herself for being so obvious.

"Uh...hello?"

"Kelly?"

"Uh, yea. Are you all right?"

"Yes, I was just anxious to find out what was going on." She admitted. "Oh, and I got my job back."

"You got your job back?" He already knew about it.

"It was the strangest thing. Doctor Bags called me and said it had all been a huge mistake and could I please come back to work. He has never been that nice to me, or anyone, before."

"Well, that's great. He must have thought it all over and changed his mind."

"That's a lot of thinking for him. I think he had some other motivation." She suspected Kelly had provided the motivation, but he wasn't admitting anything apparently.

"Oh, and they fired that security guard Simmons."

"Really, that is interesting."

"Somehow it was determined that he had been the one to let that Franklin boy escape from the facility. I heard he wasn't very happy about it."

"That's too bad." He cleared his throat. "Uh, Kay, you said you wanted to help out with the boys. Do you still want to?"

"Absolutely!" Why the heck was she was so anxious to get involved?

"Good. When we get the boys out...."

"Oh, Kelly, you're going to save them."

"Hopefully. One thing at a time though. Once we have them we need to make sure they're healthy. I know you could do it but I met a guy at the County Hospital, he was a doctor in Vietnam, but now he's doing......other things..."

"You mean Doctor Nguyen? Such a fine surgeon and they made him a janitor, shameful."

"You know him?"

"Of course. The Vietnamese community is small, but well organized in Chicago. I met him at the hospital when I was there with a patient and he introduced me to an area up on Argyle Street that has a little Vietnamese community, restaurants and shops. I miss the food sometimes." She had been *in country* for two tours after all.

"Could you contact him and put yourselves on stand-by until we make our move?"

"We'll be ready." She was so excited she was shaking, or maybe she was scared, she couldn't tell the difference at the moment.

Chapter 48: The Home

Before they could execute the plan Curtin needed to get reports from his operatives who were conducting surveillance on the Home. Nobody noticed shoe shine boys walking past with their wooden boxes slung over their shoulders. He called Mamma and found out that only Father Brown, Halloran and the little priest with the dead pan expression had been in the house overnight.

When he got to the Memorial one of the boys was there on duty. He gave his report in a very serious manner, these street boys were adults in many ways. Father Halloran had come out in his priest robes, gone to the back of the house and started the big Cadillac. He drove around to the front and Father Brown came out, getting in the back seat. When they drove off Allright took off after them. Curtin gave the boy twenty dollars and told him he did a good job, the boy didn't smile, this was a job. He thanked Curtin and took off on a little bicycle.

If Allright wasn't driving a sapphire blue, hot rod, Curtin would have had better hopes for him not being spotted. He had strict orders, don't get too close and get the hell out of there if you're spotted. Curtin didn't want to have to answer to Mamma if he got hurt.

A little before the usual arrival time, just in case, a mail truck pulled up and parked in the driveway pulling up as close to the front stairs as possible. That was Curtin's cue. He started across the street just as the mail man was taking a large mail bag out of the truck and walking it up the stairs.

The mail man rang the doorbell, tugging on his collar while he waited.

The uniform was about ten sizes too small for Patrick, the hat felt like a thimble on his head. When the door opened, Patrick looked at the little priest and almost felt sorry for him. Almost.

The priest was obviously pissed off. He was just about to give Patrick a piece of his mind when Patrick socked him in the head. Not as hard as he could. Not as hard as he wanted too. Just a little tap, with a fist the size of a cabbage, and the priest went nighty night.

Curtin arrived on the porch just as his brother was gently lowering the priest to the floor. The guy was completely unconscious. They didn't want him to bang his head and scramble his brains before they found out where the kids were.

Chapter 49: 47th & Lake Park Avenue

As long as I was on stand-by, I figured I would try my luck at the bus stops in the morning. I had two choices, start at the lake or at the other end, which went all the way to Cicero, Illinois. I headed for the lake. There was a bus terminal at the end of the line, where they turned around and went back west on 47th Street.

After a couple of hours of talking with anyone who would talk to me, including the various bus drivers, I had scored a big fat goose egg. The White Sox were playing and I had my little transistor radio to listen to the game when it started, but that wasn't for another hour so I decided to go for a walk and get a bottle of RC.

Lake Park Avenue parallels the Illinois Central railroad tracks, Lake Shore Drive, and ultimately Lake Michigan itself. Even though there is a million dollar view of the lake, you could live anywhere along Lake Park Avenue for a pocket full of change.

I was walking down the street aiming for the Lake Park Grocery, an ingenious name, past dilapidated two flats, some abandoned to the junkies with broken windows and no doors, when I saw two people that I should have figured would be together.

Lorna Palmer, Franklin's mother, came out of the Lake Park Grocery. She looked so different from when I had met her at the station when I had booked her son that I almost missed it. I could see she had been playing a part then. A long arm held the door open for her and followed her out onto the street. Her shadow looked a lot like the security guard from the Audy Home, Simmons.

The store took up about four lots. There was no parking for customers, but you wouldn't leave your car unattended around here anyway. The windows were covered with huge white paper signs advertising chitterlings, pig's feet, neck bones and other delicious sounding items. Actually, I loved red beans and rice made the traditional way, with neck bones.

Simmons saw me first, maybe he was a better body guard than a door guard. He nudged Lorna Palmer and she stopped, staring at me, not knowing what to do upon seeing me in such an unexpected place.

"Hello, Mrs. Palmer." I smiled and walked up to her. She had a huge purse that she was trying to close and hide behind her at the same time.

"What are you doing here?"

"Why I'm looking for Franklin. And I'd like to talk to you about him, among other things." I glanced at her purse.

"Well, I gots to go clean a house now and I ain't got no time to talk." She was putting on that cleaning lady act for me again but I wasn't going for it. She sure wasn't dressed to scrub floors. This woman was no cleaning lady.

"Well, you can tell your employer that I stopped to talk to

you and they can call me if they don't believe you." I had a
new track to roll on now.

"First, and most importantly, I'd like for you to bring
Franklin in and we can process him and get him some
counselling."

"Counselling, shit. You want to put him in jail."

"Of course he will be held in custody, but it won't be a
jail with adults. He isn't going to do adult time on this, I
promise."

"You promise." She couldn't have been more sarcastic. I had
no intention of throwing the key away on Franklin. He was
a murderer yes, but a disturbed child at the same time.

"Let me alone, I haven't done anything, and I have to be on
my way." She hadn't even acknowledged Simmons, who was
a respectful pace behind her, obviously ready to jump if she
gave the command. And she did. Not with words, just a look
over her shoulder when she tried to brush past me.

Simmons telegraphed a punch from Cincinnati, by the time
it was going in my direction I had already stepped inside it.
I stomped down on his instep so hard I could hear the little
bones in his foot crunch. It sounded like stepping on a bag
of potato chips. That is until the screaming drowned out all
the other sounds on the street.

I grabbed Lorna firmly by the sleeve, then guided her over
to the doorway of the store where the screaming wasn't so
loud.

"What did you do to him?"

"Must have accidentally stepped on his foot. He'll be all right." And every time it gets cold in Chicago, he's going to remember this day. That's what he deserved for trying to finger me for Franklin's escape.

"Franklin isn't the only thing that we need to talk about." She looked at me suspiciously when I said that.

"We need to talk about the pimp, the policy man, and the dope peddler. I'm thinking they might all be the same man, your boss." She just stood there although I could feel her stiffen when I spoke.

"I have nothing to say to you, sir." Although she had just said volumes. I let go of her arm.

"Look....Lorna....I don't really care about Johnny Slater, or what's in your purse. That's not my job. I'm a Youth Officer." When I mentioned Slater that hit a cord.

"I just want Franklin to come in. Do the right thing for your son. You can't hide him forever. What kind of life can he have unless he goes through the process and gets some help? Believe me, I want to help him." I didn't say I promise, it didn't go over very well the first time I promised her something.

She walked away ignoring the big man writhing on the pavement. I didn't. I stood over him where he had managed to sit up on the curb. "This is over now, man. You lied on me and we had it out. It's a big city, I don't want to see you again. Understand?" I said it like I thought Cecil Washington would say it. Simmons nodded, probably glad it was over. Me too, I was making enough enemies.

Chapter 50: Hyde Park

Lorna walked around until she was sure Kelly wasn't following her, then crossed 47th Street south bound. 47th Street was like the dividing line between the Hyde Park mansions that had been built more than fifty years ago and the Ghetto. The *White Flight* real estate crooks couldn't budge these people, Hyde Park held its value regardless of what was going on around it.

Johnny Slater lived in an apartment building on Ingleside Avenue, on the edge of the high rent neighborhood. As soon as Lorna turned down Ingleside she knew he wasn't home. The big sky blue duce-and-a-quarter wasn't parked in front of his building. No one ever parked in his spot or messed with his car when it was there. He had been known to shoot out his apartment window at people who touched his car.

When she turned back towards 47th the big blue convertible came around the corner. Seeing Lorna, Johnny pulled over to the curb and motioned for her to get in. The street was narrow, one lane south bound. When they drove past his apartment building, he owned the entire twelve flat, Johnny glanced at the doorway to see if any kids were loafing around, one of his pet peeves.

There was just one kid standing there ringing one of the doorbells. His back was to the street. He'd better really be visiting someone or he would get his own doorbell rung, by Johnny. One of the routines for burglars was to ring doorbells first to see who was home, then break into the unoccupied apartments.

"What's so important that you coming to my house? And where is Simmons?" Lorna filled him in on her encounter with Kelly. He looked in his mirror a couple of times while the story unfolded. He was especially interested in the dope peddler comment, though not interested at all in what had happened to Simmons.

He was worried but tried to brush it off, focusing on something else. "Why don't you give up that boy of yours? He's dumb as a dirt, ain't gonna amount to nothing but a jail bird, the cop's right about that. Although I'd like to get my hands on him first for what he did to my girl." He owned people.

"That whore got what she deserved. Sexing a young boy like that." Lorna defended her son, as she always would.

"It's your fault, Johnny. You put her downstairs from me. I told you I didn't want no tricks going on in my building." She owned a building too, just not a very valuable one.

"I don't give a shit what you want. You just do your job and shut up. And keep that retarded son of yours away from me." She knew he couldn't fire her. She ran the whole policy operation, but she hadn't signed on for dope and she told him.

"Why did you start that dope peddling anyway?"

"I had some........clients who wanted to trade heroin for some ass. Then they wanted to trade it for money. The shit is pure and they got no idea how much it's worth on the street so I couldn't pass it up. I ain't peddling, I just double the price and pass it on. Been working pretty well. Plus they have other things to sell. There's a lot of money to be made here."

He looked down at his clothes. He was wearing a blue suit that matched his Duce, white leather shoes that matched the leather interior, a yellow silk shirt and floral tie. Hell, he was wearing a thousand dollars' worth of clothes, not counting the beaver skin Fedora on the back seat. That alone had cost him $250.

Lorna was unimpressed with Slater. He was just another user. She was trying to get ahead in a place that was designed to keep you down. Johnny could peddle his dope or girls or whatever he wanted, but he was just a middle man. The guys who Johnny reported to with the policy proceeds knew who she was, they also knew that she made the cash, Johnny was just the flash.

To show he was the boss he didn't even drive Lorna home, instead dropping her off where he had picked her up near the corner on Ingleside and then driving to the middle of the block and pulling into his permanent parking spot. He looked up at the sky to determine whether he thought it would rain or not, decided against it and left the top down. It was easier to get his ever increasing bulk out of the car that way too.

It was then that he noticed the kid still standing in the doorway pretending to ring doorbells. He knew he had seen him here when he drove by before so the kid was up to no good. Time for a little discipline. He walked up behind the kid and grabbed his shoulder spinning him around. He didn't even see the butcher knife until he was stabbed, the blade buried in his stomach up to the handle.

"I should have killed you instead." Franklin Palmer said.

Johnny Slater bellowed like a bull, turning back towards his car but making it only a couple of steps to the parkway before falling face first onto the handle of the knife, snapping it off. He laid still, dead as the grass he way lying on.

Franklin stood there looking down at the yards of blue fabric that had billowed out around the large man. He didn't even notice when his mother walked up, taking a firm grip on his arm, guiding him down the street. They walked several blocks before Franklin came to his senses enough to wonder where they were going and he asked his mother.

"We're going to the Police Station." She had not let go of his arm, and was not about to. Franklin walked calmly next to his mother like they were out for a casual stroll.

Chapter 51: The Home

The little priest was sitting in an ornate chair with a high back. His head was slumped forward and Curtin had to keep propping him up. There was a needle in his right arm that had a short hose attached to it. There was a syringe with a hypodermic needle plugged into the other end of the little hose.

"Ok Father, time to wake up now, I have a few questions." Curtin was sing song in his speech. The little priest lolled his head back and forth, slowly recovering from the sock in the head that Patrick had given him.

They were still in the Home for Boys. Patrick was watching the front, hoping Halloran and Brown would come back before they were through questioning the little priest. Curtin was hoping they didn't come back. Letting Patrick beat them to death was too easy, as much as his brother would enjoy it.

When the priest looked up, his vision began to clear, Curtin pushed the plunger on the syringe a little. After a few minutes, he gave him a little more and started to talk to the priest. The little priest was naked. He had scars from the ritual of the Stigmata that the priests subjected themselves to. Scars on both hands and feet and a line carved into the bottom rib on the right side that had healed into an ugly gash.

All this guy wore was a coarse brown robe, sandals, and the rosary. He had one other thing. Curtin looked over to an antique side table where the robe had been thrown. On the edge there was a little jar of Vaseline that the priest kept in his pocket.

"Father, where are the boys?"

"The boys? The boys are here at home." The scopolamine was working but Curtin had to get the priest to think about the boys and where they were now. They had been at the *Home* for so long.

"No father, you moved the boys. Remember? Where did you move them?"

"Cots, we need cots. Can't have them sleeping on the floor."

"That's right Father, we can't have them sleeping on the floor." Curtin pushed the plunger a little more.

"Where are the cots supposed to be delivered Father?"

"To the Facility."

"Where is the Facility Father? We need to go there and bring the cots for the boys."

"On Halsted. The Graves Registration Facility." There it was. Curtin wondered what a huge overdose of scopolamine would do to the priest.

"He's going to burn them."

"What? Who's going to burn them?"

"Father Brown. He says they're heathens." The little priest began to cry. Curtin had only one more question.

"Why do you carry that jar of Vaseline Father? Is it for having sex with the boys?"

"Nooooo.......Umm." His subconscious didn't want him to admit to his monstrous behavior, but the drug was compelling him admit to what he was, he nodded his head, unable to lie.

It was enough for Curtin. He pushed the plunger on the syringe all the way home. The priest stiffened, turned out a huge dose of the drug was fatal.

The little priest was really sliding out of the chair now that he was dead and Curtin wanted to send a message to Brown and Halloran so he used the rosary to tie the dead priest to the high back chair.

The body slumped, but his head was held erect by the beads around his neck. It was frightening. Curtin approved. He took a camera out of his work bag and snapped a picture.

Chapter 52: Lake Park Avenue

When I was a rookie this area was my beat. There were shootings almost every night starting with my first day; after the sun had gone down on a hot summer day there was a shooting on the ground floor at 4040 South Oakenwald, a federal housing project. A young man had been getting off the elevator when he was hit in the head with a blast of OO Buck shot from a sawed off shotgun. I got the call.

Upon arrival there were so many people milling around it looked like the entire 12 story building had emptied out. I was working a one man car, that was supposed to be forbidden in this area, but I was a rookie so I had no say in the matter. The guy I was supposed to be working with was so drunk they put him in a cell to sober up, making it look like there were two men on the car, on paper.

The people were blocking traffic so I left the rotating blue light going on the top of the squad car when I reached under the dash board for the radio, unhooked the microphone and called for help before I even got out of the car. When I approached the body I had to step over vomit that other spectators had left after viewing the carnage. At least I didn't add to it.

The boy's head was split in half but still attached at the neck, no face. No brains, the skull was scooped out like a melon, the brains and face were blasted all over the inside of the elevator. Even though this building had an unobstructed view of the lake the higher you lived the lower your status. The most well connected tenants lived on the lowest floors. With this elevator out of order for the time being, many people would be walking up twelve flights while the remaining elevator chugged slowly up and down stopping at every floor.

Seeing that I was alone people started voicing their opinions about the poor police protection in the building, that the other elevator didn't work either, and whatever, then others joined in and the crowd started to blame me for all the woes that plagued the ghetto.

I couldn't do anything to help the victim, but it was increasingly evident that I needed to do something to help myself. I started to edge my way back to the squad car, and the radio. Seeing my retreat, a few of the young men saw an opportunity to get even with the *Man* and tried to cut me off from the driver's door.

I pushed a couple of guys out of my way and put the key in the trunk lock. With my left hand I opened the trunk, with my right I grabbed the shotgun from the rack by the slide. Holding it up over my head, I chucked a round in the chamber. It was a sound that commanded respect. I brought the barrel down to head level.

"Anybody want to look like that asshole in the hallway, just step right up, I got plenty of shells." That cleared a nice area around me while I waited for back-up.

My little scuffle with Simmons reminded me of the rules in the Lake Park neighborhood. *You either run it, or you run.*

The store I was entering was owned by a guy named Omar. He was from Pakistan. That didn't mean shit on Lake Park Avenue.

Omar remembered me though, smiling a big hello. He couldn't have missed the little scene out front, probably not wanting to get his toes stepped on too. I had only come this way for a bottle of pop, but I had another thought when I walked over to the cooler and pulled out a sixteen ounce bottle of Royal Crown Cola.

Omar tried to wave away my quarter when I put it on the counter, but I wasn't letting him buy me anything. He had a few customers so I sipped my soda while he waited on them, looking at some of the items on the shelves. I picked up a can of powdered infant formula.

When the last customer left, I held up the can. "Omar, you have any customers that just had a baby?"

"There are many babies around here. I sell a lot of that." He'd been on this street twenty years and still had a heavy accent.

"I'm not asking about how many babies there are around here. I want to know if you have a customer that just had a baby a day or so ago." He didn't answer. He didn't want to get involved.

"I'm looking for a woman who looked pregnant, but she didn't act like she was pregnant." Boom, he knew exactly who I was talking about, still no comment. I wasn't going to let that happen. I knew how to deal with Omar.

"Omar, we have two choices here. One is where you're a hero. The other one is where you're in jail."

"You cannot threaten me! You cannot come into my store to threaten me…I know nothing of what you want! I have done nothing, you cannot put me in jail for doing nothing!" I'd bet that where he came from they did it all the time.

"Oh Omar. I thought you remembered me. I remember you. For instance, I know that you have six illegal Mexican's who live upstairs in that little crawl space, who clean and restock your store every night, I know that you also swap them out for a new crew every month. But more interesting is the lady who just left, Lorna, I didn't see her carrying any groceries, which tells me that she was in here for something else. Like gambling or dope."

"Dope! Dope! I no dope!"

"All right, fine. You're not selling dope, just policy." He didn't say anything.

"At any rate, I'm going to make the choice for you. I choose for you to be a hero." I smiled my most sinister grin. "Where is she, Omar?"

Seeing the only path that I was allowing him to follow, he deflated a bit, pointing across the street.

"I know she is not having baby. She has big belly but not pregnant, I have six children, I know a pregnant. Then yesterday she comes in for buy baby formula, and she has baby. I see it but could not believe it."

"You were right. You shouldn't believe it. Let me use your phone will you, hero?"

Chapter 53: The Home

When Father Brown and Halloran returned from their meeting with the Cardinal, which had been followed by a gourmet dinner at Chez Paul, they noticed that all the lights were off but didn't think anything was amiss. It was likely Francis was in the Chapel disciplining himself, a daily ritual for him.

When they started up the stairs however they saw the front door was wide open. Having spent time in war zones they immediately separated, using the brick structure on either side of the doorway to protect themselves from any impending attack.

Brown gestured Halloran through the doorway first. Halloran had a Walther PPK in his hand, he led with it. The foyer was dark. It being after ten o'clock. Moving quickly out of the doorway, to present less of a silhouette to any combatants inside, Halloran moved along the wall watching something that was in the center of the room that he could just barely make out in the dim light coming from the street.

He moved all the way around the room, clicking the light switch on the wall outside the dining room door. When he saw the naked man in the chair he gasped.

"Turn that light off!" Father Brown was trying to quickly close the front door to keep any passers-by from seeing the horrible sight. It didn't bother him though. The light stayed on, Halloran was frozen in place at the sight of Father Francis.

His eyes were open wide, staring up, mouth gaping in a silent scream. The Crucifix on the rosary hung down his chest like a tie. The neck was quite elongated due to his body weight pulling against the rosary beads that were wrapped around his throat, tying him to the chair.

"Put that gun away, get him out of that ridiculous position." Brown swept past Father Francis as though he was a potted plant. He had a small Derringer two shot pistol in his hand. He was so arrogant, he thought two shots would be all he would ever need. They quickly cleared the building. They didn't find anyone, but they did find that some of their files were missing.

"What should I do with Francis?" Halloran had seen many things, but this was frightening, more so because the body was in their foyer.

"Put his robe back on him, and put him down in the old coal bin in the basement, for now."

Halloran gently removed the rosary from Father Francis' neck, lifting him out of the chair. He thought about the little priest and was sad for him. He was so light, Halloran could have carried him with one hand. Francis had been a disturbed man, surely, but he never really harmed the boys, or anyone for that matter. Halloran reminded himself to say a mass for Francis, since he wasn't going to get any services in the coal bin.

It wasn't until he was putting the robe back on the body that he saw the words scrawled over Francis' heart. He was shaken by the boldness of these people. Who the hell were they, what were their intentions? If they were trying to send a message, it was loud and clear. Halloran again wished he could run away like those two boys.

Halloran went back upstairs after saying a prayer over Francis. Brown was in his office with the lights off. Halloran could only see him by the ambient light streaming in through the large picture window. He wasn't making a target of himself.

"Ok." He admitted to Halloran. "It can't be that Kelly. So who is it?"

"Tomas `de Torquemada." Halloran said it. He didn't understand it.

"What are you talking about?" Brown's chair squeaked, indicating he had spun around to face Halloran.

"They wrote that on Father Francis. They wrote it with an ink pen over his heart. Obviously sending us a message."

"A message of what? That they are the Spanish Inquisition? Don't be ridiculous. They're just trying to scare us." Brown had to consider the implication, however, Torquemada was the Inquisitor General. He was the judge and jury, inflicting the harshest punishments upon those he judged as heretics.

"This place is obviously compromised. It's going to be up to you to secure it. I will have to make other accommodations." Brown had so many operations going around the world that he wasn't going to let this little set back bother him. However if there was a possibility of additional loss of personnel, it wasn't going to be him.

"Don't worry, we will find these people, they will pay dearly. I hated to lose those files though, that was all the material we had collected to use as leverage on the priests who uh.....used our services." Brown was always thinking ahead, Halloran was wondering if he was Torquemada's next victim.

"If we are going to get ahead of them we have to figure out who we are dealing with first. We have to consider all possibilities. Hell, it could be that Johnny Slater, he may think he's going to squeeze a better deal out of us, if he scares us a little." Brown wished it was the blacks, he hated them so much would love to show a few of them how to really torture a man.

Halloran disagreed. "No, I don't think it was him. Although, I haven't been able to reach him. He loves the deal we gave him. He thinks that we don't know the value of the heroin. I don't think he would do anything to screw that up. He wants to buy guns from us too. No, this has to do with our boys. Kelly is definitely part of it. He started it, him and that nurse."

Thinking of the big picture, Brown agreed. "Call Julian and Paul, tell them to dispose of those boys immediately." It was a grim decision, but it had to be made. They were heathens after all. Heathens that could make a lot of trouble for Brown if they fell into the wrong hands.

"Yes Father." Halloran was sad that it had come to this. After what had happened to Francis, he could hardly bear the thought that the boys would be terminated and cremated at the facility. He loved those boys, but he knew it had to be done.

This Torquemada character had surely burned up the two special ops agents he had sent after Kelly. Now they had come into their home and killed Francis. They had the boy Poc. Torquemada was one step ahead of them regardless of what Brown wanted to believe.

Chapter 54: 4634 S. Lake Park Avenue

Kelly headed for the building that Omar had pointed to across the street from the Lake Park Grocery. Considering the condition of some of the buildings on this street this one was in pretty good shape. There was even a little grass growing inside the chain link fence that surrounded the front yard. Kelly let himself in the front gate, went up the short flight of stairs to the front doors, there were two bells. He rang them both.

A man in a People's Gas Company uniform came to the door on the right, the one for the first floor. He was medium sized, his uniform was that of a supervisor, not a ditch digger. He asked Kelly what he wanted before Kelly could say anything. This was his house, this man had no reason to fear the police, which Kelly obviously was.

"Excuse me, Sir." Kelly was not about to disrespect anyone who answered the door to his own home. "Sorry to bother you. But I was wondering if someone at this location just had a baby."

The man broke out in a big grin saying proudly, "Me! Man, I just had a baby. A little boy, 6 pounds, 9 ounces." There wasn't any doubt that this man thought he had just become a father.

"Well, that's great!" Kelly smiled back at him, not knowing how to approach the matter.

"You want to see him?" That would be one way, Kelly thought.

"Sure." The man stepped into his house and Kelly followed him into a clean well-furnished living room, then into the kitchen where a woman was feeding a baby at the kitchen table. She was smiling when she looked up but stopped when she saw Kelly. He recognized her from the hospital.

When he saw the visual exchange between his wife and Kelly the man turned to Kelly and said, "How did you know that someone in this house had just had a baby?"

"That's not really important Mister......Turner." Kelly read the name off of the man's shirt. He turned to the woman.

"Ma'am, my name is Kelly, Jim Kelly. You know why I'm here. This is a tough situation for both of us. How do you think we should proceed?"

She sighed, and looked down at the baby as if it were the last time, which it probably would be. The baby was busily sucking down a bottle of formula. Kelly could see the kitchen was stocked with baby supplies. Off to his right he could see the baby's room with a crib and changing station. There were mobiles hanging over the crib, stuffed animals everywhere.

She looked up at her husband and said, "Clarence, this isn't our baby. I lost our baby three months ago. I didn't know what to do, you were so happy...we were so happy." She started to cry and her husband went over to her, knelt down next to the chair, taking her hand. Kelly wanted to leave, to give them some privacy, but there was a crime involved here also. The interest and safety of the child came first, regardless of the circumstances.

It was late by the time Kelly had finished his paperwork. After his phone call to the unit, half the police force descended on the area around 47th and Lake Park Avenue.

Wojohowski and Toolis were the hero's, although they surreptitiously gave Kelly the wink while they were explaining to the news reporters how they had tracked down the kidnapper after their investigators compiled reports of women who had recently given birth.

They went on and on until the Deputy Superintendent, who had shown up to take ultimate credit for saving this child, pushed them aside. There were also cameras in the Lake Park Grocery where Omar was happily boosting his business with free advertising.

Barbara Cunningham readily confessed to the crime. After she had lost her baby the emotional strain was too much for her. She started to think about ways to replace the child she had lost. She didn't want anyone to know she had lost her baby so she pretended she was still pregnant. She continued to go to the hospital for regular checkups but just walked around the building, checking things out. She gradually increased her baby bump. She talked to people about her upcoming event. Part of her thought she was still pregnant.

When the day came, the day she would use as the baby's birthday, she put on the nurse's uniform she had purchased that matched the ones from the hospital, went into the maternity ward and just took the baby from the mother's arms telling her the baby needed a bath and would be returned shortly.

Cunningham had already chosen the victim, when the baby boy was born earlier in the week. She had just picked him out while looking through the window of the viewing room as though she could have had anyone she chose. He had been the pick of the litter.

She changed clothes in the basement and went out through the Emergency Room where it was chaotic all the time. She had even walked right past a guard, openly carrying the baby, with a big smile on her face.

And she might have gotten away with it had Kelly not seen her reaction when she was struck with that door in the hospital. He was sure Omar would have kept his suspicions to himself, as long as she kept buying the infant formula from him.

Chapter 55: Area 3 Youth Office

The paper work Kelly was finishing wasn't even related to the kidnapping. He had ended up giving the pinch to the other guys in the unit along with two police women who were caring for the baby. The Youth Division was the only unit that had female personnel. Maureen Taylor and Barb Garwin were actually sworn personnel, carrying guns and stars, although the stars said *Police Woman* on them, instead of *Patrolman*.

Kelly had come up to the squad room prepared to get started on the paperwork for the Cunningham arrest when he saw Lorna Palmer and Franklin sitting next to his desk. When he explained who they were to Toolis, the sergeant was delighted to have also caught an escaped murderer. He told Kelly to focus on that while everybody else handled the kidnapping.

Kelly didn't care. You didn't get extra pay for being a hero on this job. After talking with Lorna Palmer, Kelly had called the Homicide desk upstairs to check on something Lorna confessed to him.

"Hello? Yea, Dombrowski? Kelly. Yes, from the kiddy cops. I just wanted you to know that I found that former witness turned murderer, Franklin Palmer, so in case you were looking for him to help me out...Oh, you weren't? Well, did you ever turn that pimp over to the Vice Control Division? I heard he was...."

"Dead? How did that happen? Do you need me to come up there and find the killer for you again?"

"Yea, well, fuck you too." Kelly hung up and looked over to where Lorna and her son were sitting.

Lorna was waiting patiently with Franklin, having confessed to what had happened to Johnny Slater, they didn't know what was going to happen, but they had come clean, Kelly appreciated that. He also had been serious when he had told Mrs. Palmer that he wouldn't let Franklin do adult time.

Kelly had a big decision to make. Dombrowski had told him that Johnny Slater was murdered during an armed robbery in front of his house. He had been selling heroin and had paid the price of trafficking in narcotics. There were no suspects in custody and it didn't sound as though they were going to great lengths to find any.

Kelly went over and sat at his desk, still unsure of what to do when Frankie Bartuca called out to him to pick up line one.

"Kelly." It was Curtin.

"Kelly, we're going tonight to get them out. Call your girlfriend and have her meet us at Mr. Washington's house."

"She's not my girlfriend."

"Whatever. Get your ass over to Ma's house as soon as you can." That decided what he was going to do with Franklin Palmer.

He asked Bartuca if he would take Franklin over to the Audy Home. Frankie, who lived right near there, was happy to do something for Kelly after Kelly put him on the paper to get credit for the kidnapping arrest.

When he told Lorna that Bartuca was going to take Franklin to the Audy Home, she looked a question at him.

"I made a promise, if we had to get into this other thing it would prevent me from keeping it, so we'll just forget about Johnny Slater." Her eyes filled up with tears. Kelly was actually glad that Johnny Slater was off the board. He would have ended up the same way sooner or later.

To Franklin he said, "And when Officer Bartuca takes you to the Audy Home, stay there this time, will you?"

"Don't worry, Mr. Kelly," Lorna said, clutching her big purse that still had hundreds of dollars' worth of gambling proceeds in it. "We're going straight there. Come Franklin, Officer Bartuca?"

Chapter 56: Fallen Heroes Crematory, 43rd & Halstead

Father Paul looked at Julian when he hung up the phone. He didn't have to tell Julian what the phone call was about. They had been instructed to terminate the eight boys and have Sergeant Goddard cremate them in the ovens that they used to cremate fallen soldiers from Vietnam who had not been claimed by family.

"We'll say a mass and give them all communion before." Julian said. Paul didn't argue, neither one of them wanted to do this, but orders from Father Brown were not negotiable. They didn't want to end up in the blast furnace themselves.

They were upstairs on the second floor of the facility which was a large brick structure that had once been a meat packing house. After a tax seizure Brown had bought the building from the city for a dollar.

Father Antonin Brown had excellent contacts within the government and around the world. When it was learned that the bodies of service men killed in Vietnam were piling up without any family or friends to claim them, or to bury them, the government was delighted to sign onto Father Brown's plan.

Fallen soldiers who were unclaimed were now sent to Chicago, to the Fallen Heroes facility on Halsted. There, the coffins were unsealed, the bodies were cremated, the ashes then placed in official looking boxes and sent to Washington where they were buried with proper ceremony at Arlington or sent to other military cemeteries around the country.

Brown's ingenious idea being that they could bury the cremated remains of a hundred men in the space that it would take to bury one body in a coffin. The military cemeteries were reaching capacity, more bodies coming back from Vietnam every day.

The clincher for the government was that Father Brown and his "Fallen Heroes Ministries", as he called the nonprofit he had started just for this program, worked for free. There were Army Graves Registration Division personnel on site who did the work, but all of the paperwork said **Fallen Heroes Ministries**. Father Brown claimed the unclaimed bodies. It was a perfect solution for the government and they had the Catholic Church to cover up the fact that our fallen servicemen were being treated so disgracefully.

However no one in the government or even the eight regular army soldiers that worked at the facility knew what was in specially marked coffins that came from Hawaii. The typical shipment of coffins were all identical, with a slight exception on one of them. Only the priests and Sergeant Goddard knew what was in the coffins marked with a red slash. It wasn't a mark that was too obvious, it looked like the coffin had banged into an object that was painted red and a little rubbed off.

When they took the truck to the airport to pick up the

coffins on Wednesdays, Goddard was always there to sign for them and supervise loading the army 2.5 ton transport vehicles. Goddard would also find the one that had the red slash on it. That one would not be opened until after the shift was ended and the regular army guys had gone home.

Then his old buddies from Special Ops would come and help him with the grisly task of taking the heroin out of the bodies, where it had been secreted. That they were priests now didn't surprise Goddard. Some of those guys had been way out there.

When Brown and Halloran had come to him with the scheme, he was delighted to sign on. Goddard had been dumped into Graves Registration after being an unproven suspect involving some civilians who had been raped and murdered after a night of drinking. He figured there would be no more advancement for him anyway, so he may as well make a little extra money to save for retirement. He only had a few years to go to collect his pension.

Chapter 57: Curtin's Kitchen

When I got there, I had to stand because there were so many people sitting around Ma Curtin's kitchen table. Beside Curtin, brothers Patrick and Danny were present, though apparently Michael and John wouldn't be party to what was going down. I didn't know the plan, but I didn't need to know it to know that we didn't need a politician or a priest, at least not yet.

At the head of the table sat the brother-in-law Nicky Fellino, flanked by two of the scariest Sicilians I'd ever seen, all three were dressed in black suits. They weren't big tough guys or karate looking guys. They were just scary.

"You're late."

"Well, I had to work. I......"

"Yea, yea, we know you found that kidnapped kid. You win a cookie." Curtin was having fun pulling my leg, everybody was smiling, not the Sicilians.

"Thank you for your support," I said to the group. "I did find out something about Johnny Slater."

That got Curtin's attention. The others didn't really know about Slater. "Yes?" He prompted. I had to give it up without any fan fair or pats on the back.

"He's now the ex-Johnny Slater."

"Really. That saves us a step. Although I would have liked to have talked to him beforehand. Kind of hard to now." That got smiles all around. "Did you kill him?"

"What? I didn't kill anybody." I said surprised. I did know more than I was sharing. I knew who killed Slater. But that would stay with me. Curtin looked at me as though he knew I wasn't telling all, then shrugged it off, wanting to get back to the topic.

"Did you talk to your girlfriend?" This was getting old.

"Yes, and she's not my girlfriend. If you don't believe me, ask her when you see her. I told her to meet us at Washington's house. He's supposed to be expecting all this, right?" I gestured around the table at the odd fellow conspiracy that was going on.

"All set. Don't worry." I hated it when he said *don't worry*. When I heard the plan, that made me worry even more.

Chapter 58: Fallen Heroes Crematory, the Rescue

We set out for the building on Halsted Street in three vehicles. Somewhere Curtin had acquired a Military Police Captain's uniform, including a Sam Browne belt with side arm. He also had commandeered an olive green Army Military Police cruiser, complete with lights and decals. It even had white numbers painted on the front and rear. I hoped those numbers weren't on a stolen vehicle list.

I didn't say anything when he handed me my uniform, even though he was a captain and I was going to be a sergeant. I wondered how many years we could get in Leavenworth for this.

The Italian branch of the assault team was driving, appropriately, a hearse. Now the black suits made sense. Pat and Danny were in Curtin's car, in case we had to dump the army vehicle. We cruised our little caravan towards the old Stock Yards neighborhood.

The building had a loading dock that fronted the street. That made it easier for trucks to pick up meat from the facility when it had been a lamb processing plant. We pulled up to the dock. The four corrugated metal rollup doors were all closed.

The hearse backed up to the dock looking like they were expecting to pick up a passenger. Curtin and I climbed the stairs on the side where there was a metal door that was illuminated by a large flood light just above it. When Curtin pressed the button on the intercom, a loud bell could be heard clanging inside the building. He leaned on it until I was ready to tell him to stop, I could only imagine how it sounded inside.

"Who is it?" an annoyed voice sounded from the little speaker above the button.

"Captain Collins, US Army, Graves Registration Division. We are here to pick up a body that was sent here by accident. You were contacted this afternoon instructing you to have...uh......Private Richard Herzog ready for pick-up." Curtin hesitated, pretending he was reading the name from the clipboard he was holding, then he smiled over at me, obviously very proud of his impersonation of an army captain.

"We're not open." The same voice came out of the little speaker. Curtin had his officer's cap pulled down, I couldn't see his eyes because of the overhead light, but I didn't have to. I knew that was not the answer he was expecting.

"This is a military installation and I am a captain in the United States Army. This facility is not, I repeat, not closed to me. It will be open right goddamn now or you better have an officer with a higher rank in there to tell me different. Am I making myself clear?"

As an afterthought, he added. "And get your ass out here and talk to me face to face before I have this goddamn door knocked down and order my sergeant to drag your ass out here." I didn't like the way this was going, mostly because I was the sergeant.

There was a lot of clanking and lock turning, finally the heavy door opened. We had brought some stuff to actually knock the door down if we had to, but Curtin always liked to do things the sneaky way. There was a soldier in green fatigues, with up and down sergeant stripes, standing in the doorway. It wasn't an invitation to enter.

He was a big guy, 225 pounds easy, around 35 years old, probably a lifer. He had the sleeves of his fatigue shirt rolled up to his elbows. The name tape was embroidered *Goddard*. He also had a skull with wings and a dagger through the eye tattooed on the inside of his forearm.

"I'm sorry sir. I didn't realize who you were. We get a lot of gang activity around here. It's pretty late and all the guys are gone for the day. I'm sure that in the morning we could......."

"In the morning I intend to be back at Fort Leonard Wood. Now! I want that goddamn body now!" Goddard raised himself up a little, clearly standing his ground.

"I am sorry sir. *There are to be no releases of deceased personnel except during regular hours.* That's an order from the Colonel." He said it like it was a direct quote. He was trying to raise our fake Captain with a fake Colonel.

"Nonsense. Get him on the phone." Curtin pushed past the man into a large docking area inside the warehouse. I thought Goddard was going to object, I was ready to slug him, but he just stood there a little overwhelmed by Curtin's Captain Act. He was getting better as he went along. To our right parked inside the roll up doors were two 2.5 ton army transport vehicles and two civilian vehicles.

One vehicle was a big black Fleetwood like the priests used, the other was a minivan. Along the walls on that side were long banks of metal freezer doors.

Behind the sergeant we could see stacks of metal coffins, a fork lift, stainless steel gurney tables and several conveyor belts that circled the floor area, ultimately ending up at the doors of two huge concrete boxes at the back of the building. There were pipes of all different sizes running into and out of the boxes. And if that picture hadn't been perfectly clear for me the entire place smelled like the morgue, my least favorite place/smell.

"I can't contact him now, sir. It's late and…" We were interrupted by a voice coming from a staircase to our left that went up to the second level that was built around the large central processing space. The man who was speaking was dressed in priest robes. He was walking down the metal staircase that was attached to the wall with a gentle smile on his face. I could see the rosary he was wearing around his waist.

"Gentleman. My name is Father Julian. I am the person who is in charge of this facility. It is a military facility yes, but all these bodies have been claimed by Father Antonin Brown who is our Spiritual Leader and Director. Only he can release one of our Fallen Heroes and he is not available to grant your request. It is late at night so I will take responsibility for you not being able to complete your mission. Now if you will just be on your way." All these guys looked alike. Big and strong. Powerful in bearing.

The priest had continued talking while he approached us, just finishing when he came to a halt a few feet away. Closer than he needed to be if he hadn't been trying to intimidate us. Curtin lifted his head a little and the priest looked at him more closely. Suddenly the priest's eyes refocused on Curtin, he recognized him from the Home. He also recognized the pistol with the silencer attached that Curtin had taken out of his convenient holster.

"Hello, Father. Remember me?" So much for the plan. Curtin smiled at the priest. Father Julian didn't return the gesture.

"Now I'm going to ask you both some questions and depending on your answers, we will proceed. Where are the boys?" Julian just glared at Curtin, but was smart enough to remain still. He was only a step away from Curtin, but Curtin's finger would beat him in any race.

Curtin stepped back out of Julian's reach, turning the gun barrel towards Goddard. "Sergeant, would you like to try for a get out of jail free card? Where are the boys?"

"I'm not telling you shit. You ain't no army officer." Curtin digested that, not deciding how he was going to respond.

"How about telling me how many other people, besides the little boys, there are around here?" Both men stood their ground. Suddenly Nicky and the Sicilians were in the room flanking us at the periphery of our vision.

We couldn't afford to take our eyes off of Julian and Goddard. We also couldn't afford to wait or risk harm to the boys by delay. *Pftttt......*Curtin shot Father Julian in the shoulder with the silencer. Right through the socket. The priest had no choice, but to start screaming.

There was movement above us, we looked up to see another priest emerge from the door at the top of the stairs. Curtin took aim and shot him twice, holding the weapon with two hands, ready to shoot anyone else that came out the door. The priest rolled down the stairs and didn't move when he came to rest. Curtin wasn't aiming to wound the guy like he had Julian, who was clutching his shoulder, gaping at his fellow priest who was already pumping blood into a pool around him.

Curtin tensed and almost fired again as another figure cautiously came around the edge of the doorway at the top of the stairs. I reached out to stop him, but he had already lowered the gun barrel. We both recognized the little head with a familiar haircut, first one, then another and another poked around the door jamb. Curtin turned to Father Julian.

"You're very fortunate that those boys are still alive Father Julian. I was scaring myself thinking what I would do to you if you had harmed them. If we had gone that way, I'm sure you would have agreed. Instead let me give you something for that pain." Curtin shot him in the eye, less blood.

I thought I might feel differently about Curtin's action. I knew what he was capable of. I thought I would feel guilt, spiritual remorse for killing a priest. Worse than a regular mortal sin right? Not these priests. They needed to be eradicated, not prosecuted.

On cue, Pat and Danny appeared and started up the stairs. I heard them speaking in Vietnamese to the boys. They had also been to Vietnam. The only word I could understand however was Poc. I really needed to learn some Vietnamese.

Within a few seconds the eight boys, all dressed in white tee shirts and shorts, were running down the stairs following Patrick out of the building with Danny bringing up the rear carrying a machine gun. Where the hell did he get a machine gun?

Goddard was frozen in place with his hands up in the air.

"Ok, just a few more questions sergeant." Curtin pointed the pistol at him. Goddard gulped.

"The heroin. It comes from Hawaii concealed in the bodies of dead soldiers, right?" Goddard nodded.

"The coffins with the red mark are the ones with the dope." Goddard offered. It wasn't nearly enough. Curtin took off his hat. The charade was over.

"You were going to kill those boys and burn their bodies in that furnace, weren't you?" One of the Sicilians pulled a lever on the side of one of the concrete boxes, the door slid upward revealing ferocious jets of blue gas flames enveloping the interior of the furnace. We could feel the wave of heat, where we were standing on the other side of the building.

"I wasn't going to do anything. It was them." He gestured to the bodies on the floor. "They were going to do it. I just deal with the heroin and the bodies."

"So, all you were going to do was burn the bodies for them?" Curtin glanced at Nicky and before Goddard could even nod or realize what was happening there was a click behind him, his eyes opened wide, then he slumped to the floor, the other Sicilian allowing him to slide off of the stiletto he had plunged into Goddard's heart from the back. Now I knew what was so scary about them.

Chapter 59: The Washington's

'*This is a terrible idea.*' Words Kay Miller kept repeating in her head. '*I must be crazy to get involved in this madness.*'

When Kelly called her, she was excited and eager to help. Now, not so much. She didn't even know this man, now he was possibly breaking the law, she would be counted as an accomplice. She had never even had a parking ticket, in fact she put more money in the parking meter than she needed to, in case something caused her to be delayed.

Now she was going to help rescue/kidnap eight children. That had to be a felony. Actually she didn't even know what a felony was but she felt like a criminal. Dr. Nguyen sat next to her in her little Dodge Dart while they cruised down Lake Shore Drive. He had no difficulty signing onto Kelly's crazy scheme.

She was sure that Kelly had something to do with her getting her job back, especially after he told her she should ask Dr. Bags for a week off, because she was so upset about losing her job in the first place. That sounded like the stupidest thing she had ever heard until Dr. Bags told her that he completely understood. He said she should take off all the time she needed, with pay of course. Now *that* was the stupidest thing she had ever heard.

After driving around a little they found the address. She was impressed by the huge mansions hidden here on the south side of Chicago. The one they were going to was on about an acre of land with beautiful landscaping and a circle driveway. The house was in magnificent shape. It had a wide porch with a slate roof and copper gutters. It was evident that these people valued their properties. Kelly told her to just ring the door bell and everything would be taken care of. Against her better judgement, she did so.

So far he was right. The door was answered by a large black man with a baritone voice and a captivating smile. He was dressed like a genie. He invited them in, returning the bow he received from Dr. Nguyen after they shook hands. The man, whose name was Cecil, called out over his head and Poc came bounding down the stairs two at a time. He skidded to a halt beside the gentle giant, smiling brightly when he recognized Kay and the doctor.

Dr. Nguyen started talking to the boy who had rapid fired answers. Taking the smiling Dr. Nguyen by the hand, Poc dragged him up the stairs. When Kay looked the question to Cecil, he said, "He wants to show the man his room. Boy never had a room before."

"Miss Miller, how does he say that name of his? New-Yen?" She nodded, still not saying more than her own name to the strange man, who welcomes run away children into his house.

"Poc's gonna have to share his room for a little while if those boys do they jobs tonight." He was obviously more informed than her. "Momma gonna be in her glory cooking for these kids. She can't cook that Viet food, but she can sure cook good. I ain't heard no complaints from Poc. Seems you could put about anything on top a bowl of rice and that boy would eat it." He laughed a booming laugh at his own joke. Kay smiled with him.

"Momma." When he called out towards another part of the big house a tall fair skinned woman came out of the kitchen. He introduced her as his wife Emily and asked her to make Kay a cup of tea while they waited. Kay didn't want to think about what they were waiting for.

They were sitting around the large kitchen table. Poc had returned with Dr. Nguyen and was consuming a plate full of cookies, washing it down with a glass of milk so large he had to use two hands to hold it.

"Nguyen, tell me what religion are these boys?" Cecil asked. Kay was a little shocked that the man even cared. Dr. Nguyen explained that they were Buddhists. He told Cecil a little about some of Buddha's teachings and how old Buddha was. Then Nguyen mentioned that besides being a doctor in Vietnam, he was also a Buddhist priest himself.

"Good. Good. That's just what they're gonna need. Some spiritual guidance after all what they been through. You think you could give these boys some spirit? I don't know if you all pray or whatever, but to me we're all talkin to the same Man, just in different ways. Them boys are gonna need something to help anchor them. It's a sho bet they ain't gonna want to be Cat-licks." Kay saw the wisdom in that statement.

Chapter 60: The Home

Halloran was in the office with Brown, they had drawn the blinds and turned on a low lamp when the phone rang. Halloran answered and listened, saying yes a couple of times.

"We can't come there right now but there are several of our personnel already there, they should be able to help you.....You haven't? I'll have to check on it and call you back. Oh, it is. Okay." Halloran hung up and turned to Father Brown who was waiting for an explanation.

"The facility on Halsted is on fire." Brown was expressionless, but Halloran wasn't turning his back. "They expect it to be a total loss."

"On fire? What about Julian and Paul?" He didn't ask "*what about the boys?*" The answer to Julian and Paul's whereabouts would answer that question too.

"The fire chief said that there was no one there. Do you want to go over there?"

"Are you insane? Take me to the airport." Brown had an emergency bag that was always prepared, he grabbed it and they were on the way to the airport in less than two minutes. They were at Midway Airport within half an hour.

"Get me a ticket on the next flight to Hawaii, or anywhere on the west coast." He didn't have to tell Halloran to get a first class ticket. That was understood, Brown never flew anywhere if he couldn't travel first class.

"I'll call you tomorrow and I expect answers to all questions." Brown was always in charge. Halloran thought he was nuts. He didn't have any answers now and wouldn't have any tomorrow.

"Whoever they are. They might still be in an operational mode." Halloran wasn't interested in running into whoever had been tormenting them. Torquemada be damned.

"That's the first thing I want to know. Afterwards we'll put everything we have into finding out who they are." He had no concern for Halloran's safety considering he had just been ordered to stake himself out as bait.

"And secondly, I want to know what happened to those boys. Find Paul or Julian, or Goddard, I don't care. We have to know that those boys have been disposed of." They were in front of the terminal but the clergy flag on the front fender kept the police from interrupting their conversation.

"And if they are not in the ashes of that building, I want you to find them and dispose of them yourself." Pretty tall order Halloran thought, Brown was reading his mind again.

"I will call Amsterdam and order all of the ex-military Mendalin priests to come here and protect our investment. If you're afraid to stay at the Home, you can stay at the Cardinal's mansion on North Avenue until you get some back-up. I'm sure he will be happy to put you up for a while." That didn't sound too bad to Halloran. He left the car running and went in to the ticket desk.

Chapter 61: The Washington's

The doorbell chimed like a church, it didn't just ring. Mr. Washington got up from the table. Kay followed him without asking. He didn't seem to notice. When they got into the foyer, she stood back a little while Cecil went to the ornate wooden door opening it without seeming to care who was on the other side. It was Kelly. She let out a little sigh of relief. Then she held her breath again.

He smiled at her. And just stood there.

"Well speak up Boy? I know you can talk, I've heard it before." Cecil was also a little anxious to find out what had happened. Kelly stood to the side of the door and gestured to the vehicle parked at the bottom of the steps. A man was standing by the rear door dressed like an army captain and now that she noticed, Kelly also had an army uniform on, except he was only a sergeant. Kelly gestured to the man, he opened the rear door of the car.

It was like the Clown Car Act at the circus. They just kept pouring out of the back seat. Cecil Washington started laughing and Kay realized that Mrs. Washington, Dr. Nguyen and Poc had joined the welcoming party at the door. When the boys saw Poc, it set off a celebration that caused Mr. Washington to start giving orders to take the party into the house.

Poc took the boys upstairs at the speed of sound, followed

closely by Nguyen and Kay. Kelly and Curtin went into the kitchen for a cup of coffee, feeling honored to just sit at the man's table while being served by his wife.

"You're going to need some money, Mr. Washington," Curtin said after a satisfying sip of steaming black coffee.

"I don't need no money Boy. How long you know me?"

"Sir." Curtin was afraid to argue with the man even if it was about giving him money. "I was thinking about money that should be the boy's money anyway. That priest has been using them to beg charity from all over the world, I think we may be able to get our hands on some of that money, then we can use it to get the boys settled.....or whatever you think." He chickened out at the end. Kelly was staying out of it. He was chicken at the beginning!

"Well, if what you say is true." Washington thought about it for a second then agreed. "Okay, we'll see what you can do, Boy. Then I will decide."

That was good enough for Curtin and Kelly. They knew when to shut up, sipping their coffee until Kay came into the kitchen.

"Dr. Nguyen says they're in relatively good shape. He wants to start them all on antibiotics in case of any infection, you know STD's."

"STD's?" Kelly said, not knowing what the acronym was.

"Sexually Transmitted Diseases, you dummy." Curtin said, smiling at Kay.

"He's never had one," he said to Kay, who didn't know how

to take the information. Then he added, "Thank you for doing this, Miss Miller."

Kay started to smile, then he said, "Even though Kelly said that he could get you to do anything for him." She turned on Kelly, he held up his hands in a defensive manner.

"I didn't say that. Curtin, come on. Give me a break will you?" He implored. Kay got it, let it drop, getting serious.

"Kelly, Mr. Curtin, the boys would like to thank you for saving them and ask you something." Kelly and Curtin just looked puzzled but followed her into the foyer where the boys were lined up, shortest to tallest. Dr. Nguyen was behind them smiling at their maturity.

Kelly and Curtin stopped, they surveyed the line, nine boys. They all bowed as one saying *thank you* in accented English. Kelly and Curtin were obviously embarrassed by the display of gratitude. Then, Poc spoke from his place on the end. He was the shortest.

"Kerry. You are a good friend. Thank you for save us. We would like for you to save us more. Can you save Ping and Nog?" Kelly didn't know what he was talking about.

Curtin had been listening to the tapes over and over until he knew all of the conversations practically by heart. He remembered a conversation where those two names were mentioned. Those were the two boys who were *sold* to the seminary for twenty thousand dollars.

When he asked if Ping and Nog had been sent to the seminary all the boys nodded and looked down sadly, not knowing what the seminary was but knowing it couldn't be any better than the house of horrors that they had been living in.

Curtin said, "Don't worry Poc, I'll....uh...we'll get them back, no problem. You boys just stay here do what Mr. and Mrs. Washington tell you to do, we'll take care of the rest." *Don't worry* and *no problem* in the same sentence, Kelly was extremely worried about that.

Once in the car, Kelly didn't even get a chance to say goodbye to Kay. He said to Curtin. "WE will get them back? Who's WE? You got a mouse in your pocket? Cause I've about had it playing army."

"Good. You're going to be a priest next." Kelly just shook his head, exasperated. He could only blame himself. He had started it. Just to impress a girl? Surely that was part of it.

"Well, at least I'll only have to answer to God for that crime." Kelly started pulling at his tie, taking off the uniform. Curtin had his Captain's hat on, he glanced in the mirror to make sure it was straight.

Chapter 62: The Bank

When the Drover's Bank on 35th and Morgan St. opened two days later, their first customers were a nun and a priest. The priest had a rosary around his waist and the nun had a traditional habit that looked like it had been tailored for her.

Curtin thought it probably had. When he broached the idea to his sister she was all for it and said that he didn't need to get her a nun's outfit, she had one already. Curtin didn't want to think about what kind of sex games his sister and brother-in-law engaged in.

Curtin took out the driver's license he had found in the office that had a description that matched the little priest. It identified him as Father Francis Donaldson. He showed it to the girl at the first desk that was occupied. She didn't question his credentials. Who would impersonate a priest?

Curtin had already mastered the signature on the license and he told the clerk what he wanted to do. Within the hour they had all the papers signed, Sister Elizabeth was now a signatory on all of the accounts of Father Brown's Home for Boys that were held at that bank.

They didn't know what was in the accounts, Curtin was only able to get the numbers off of some cancelled checks that were in the same drawer as the driver's license. Curtin knew this was just the bank they used for day to day business. He figured Brown had money all over the world. They needed to get somebody working on that too.

It had been Liz's idea. Since Curtin had the banking information, she suggested that they just put her on the accounts as a signatory, then she could move the money or do whatever they wanted with it once she was in control. She had gone to Notre Dame majoring in business and bookkeeping which was good for her husband because she kept him out of jail for tax fraud by doing his books.

Curtin trusted his sister absolutely so he left the rest in her hands and went to get ready to go to the seminary.

Chapter 63: The Seminary

As usual, I couldn't believe I was signing onto another one of Curtin's insane plans, but as usual I didn't have one of my own. Plus I really wanted to impress Kay Miller. Which was pathetic.

When he arrived he was in the back seat of a black Cadillac limousine that had little flags on the front fenders like ones you might see in a fancy funeral procession, except these said '*Clergy*' on them. I got in the back quickly not wanting my neighbors to see this monstrosity in front of my building.

Curtin was wearing a coarse robe like one of Brown's gang, complete with rosary and sandals.

"Where's your robe?" He said looking at my blue jeans. I held up a paper grocery bag I had brought with me. I had the itchy thing in the bag along with the hippy shoes and the beads.

"I'm not putting this shit on until I absolutely have to." At least we were going to be the same rank in this scheme.

I had been so busy looking at *Father* Curtin in his costume that I hadn't noticed who was driving. Dr. Nguyen was dressed in a black chauffeur's uniform complete with cap. A little short for the job but he looked the part.

"Hello doctor." I said.

"Not *doctor* now. Now, Nathaniel, the chauffeur." I could tell he was having fun participating in this insanity with us. This guy had been a janitor last week. What next?

When we arrived at the seminary in Villa Park, we passed through two tall iron gates that were connected to an equally high fence that ran around the huge campus. Another fence meant to keep the inmates in rather than protecting them from the evils of the world?

A large brass plaque indicated that we were entering the Pendican Catholic Seminary. I had never heard of the place, but it was busy, with acolytes dressed in black cassocks going from building to building.

We drove up to a huge three story brick building, which had probably been the original monastery. Nguyen pulled the vehicle up to the front of the building. Curtin stepped out of the limo like he was the Pope. When I got out on the other side the breeze blew up my now naked legs giving me a shiver.

Not only was I now wearing the robe, hippy sandals and rosary, we both had little decals on our hands, both backs and palms. They were a close facsimile to the scars that Father Brown and his cohorts had for real on their hands. I doubted anyone would look too closely. We weren't allowing any close scrutiny.

The front door was open. We walked in like we owned the joint. The first level seemed to be business and academic activities and was busy with end of school day turmoil. We just stood there in the foyer and acted impatient. This was picked up by several young men in black cassocks who thought better of addressing the strangers and went in different directions to report our arrival.

Soon an adult dressed in a similar black cassock came to us, introducing himself as Father Adolphus. He was tall, soft spoken with a matching placating smile.

Curtin introduced us. "I am Father Tomas `de. And this is Father Bartolomeo." Bartolomeo? Really? I wished I had picked a name in the car. Why couldn't I just be Father James?

"Tomas `de?" The priest smiled his fake smile. "Not Tomas `de Torquemada, I hope?"

Curtin didn't return the smile, instead frowning at the joke. "Actually, I am named for him." The priest gulped.

"We would see the Abbott." Curtin announced.

"Do you have an appointment?" The priest wanted to pull the words back out of the air when he said them after he saw the look on Curtin's face. Curtin held up his hand to stop the man's next comment, had there been one coming, also to show him the scar on his palm.

"Tell the Abbott that the Mendalin's are here." That was a dismissal and the priest got the message loud and clear. He started up the large staircase behind him without saying another word.

Chapter 64: The Abbott's Office

"Twenty thousand. Now." Curtin said, to the Abbott.

"But Father Brown said that we could have all the time we wanted, to see if the new boys were.....uh.....suitable for our seminary."

"That's changed. Twenty thousand, or the boys go back."

Within a few minutes we had been ushered into the Abbott's office, the reputation of Father Brown and his Mendalin Priests apparently a real door opener. The Abbott, James Antaramian, also had a shit eating grin on his face but couldn't help pulling his hand back like it had touched a snake after shaking hands with Curtin and glancing at the scars.

Welcoming us into his office, the Abbott had been gracious. Dr. Nguyen, who had entered behind us, stood by the door like a good servant, probably a part of the plan that I didn't want to know about. The Abbott had ordered tea over the phone without asking if we wanted any.

When the Vietnamese boy arrived dressed in a white bus boys' uniform I realized that he had wanted us to see how well he was treating the newbies. We did want to see them, but not for the same reason.

"It can't be done." The Abbott wasn't being gracious any longer. We were talking money now. The plan was to demand the money then when he refused we would take the boys and that would be that. Sure.

"Nathaniel," Curtin turned to Dr. Nguyen. "Go get the boys and put them in the car."

"You can't do that! Who the hell do you think you are?" The Abbott was furious. He got up from his desk, as though he were bringing the power of God down upon us. It probably impressed the students. We remained sitting in two soft leather chairs with the tea tray on an ornate table between us.

Curtin crossed his legs and leaned back, though not that intimidating with bare legs and feet, he added to Nguyen, "And Nathaniel, you are authorized to use any means necessary to acquire...........uh Father Brown's property."

"Yes, Father," Dr. Nguyen turned and left the room like a man on a mission.

Curtin turned to the Abbott who was frozen in place, not usually faced with *any means necessary* situations at the school. "As to who I am, I am Father Tomas 'de of the Order of Mendalin Missionaries."

"Okay fine. I'll take this up with Father Brown when he returns." We had explained, over tea, that Father Brown was ministering to the orphans in Vietnam at the moment and couldn't be reached.

"Okay, fine," Curtin said mockingly. "And until that time the boys go with me."

"No, I'll write you a check." He sat down and opened the

drawer in front of him taking out a large leather bound book.

"What?" Curtin slipped then caught himself. "Oh. Fine, that will be twenty thousand." Twenty thousand, we didn't want the money. We wanted the boys. Curtin was sure that they wouldn't be able to come up with twenty grand at the drop of a hat. Another plan down the drain.

The Abbott tore the check out and slid it across the desk contemptuously as if saying, *"This isn't over Father Tomas `de."*

Then he added sarcastically, "Tomas `de? Who are you named for? Torquemada?"

"Why does everyone keep asking me that?" Curtin said, sweeping up the check and leaving without another word for the Abbott or his tepid tea.

When we reached the first floor, Dr. Nguyen was there, with four Vietnamese boys, somehow he had come up with two additional boys. We just stared at him, stunned. He smiled.

Curtin didn't miss a beat, it took only a few seconds to tell Nguyen what had happened and give him instructions to give to the boys. Couldn't be a very good plan if Curtin had thought it up while we were coming down the stairs. And it wasn't.

Chapter 65: Goldblatt's

Kay was thinking about calling Doctor Bags and just quitting. She felt bad loading work on others when she was on a fake vacation. Then she thought about the 10th Floor lake view apartment that she rented in the Meadow Lakes Building and thought she might wait a while before quitting. Apparently Bags wasn't looking for her, she had a tape machine on her phone and he had left no messages.

Mrs. Washington had forbidden her from spending any money, after she had suggested some of the things that the boys needed and offering to go buy them. The Washington's supplied everything.

When Dr. Nguyen wanted to put the boys on antibiotics, Cecil had merely called a pharmacy on his beat and had the pills delivered, no prescription needed. She wanted to help but found that everything was being covered, then she had found something that she do.

Cecil had come up with a yellow school bus somewhere. It was parked out in the driveway. It was a small one and had Mt. Zion Baptist Church written on the sides. Kay had immediately volunteered to be the driver for the gang. She had driven ambulances in Vietnam, even doing it under fire. A school bus would be a piece of cake she told Cecil, who tossed her the keys.

They also had an idea for a school, of sorts. The house had a big basement so they decided to create a classroom. They already had Emily who was a retired teacher. She had boxes of school books, stacked to the ceiling, down there. The boys were eager to start school. Kay didn't understand what they meant about opening envelopes all day at the Home but didn't inquire, not wanting to dwell on an obvious unpleasant memory.

Mrs. Washington decided that the first thing they needed was a trip to the Goldblatt's Department Store on the corner of 63rd and Halsted, the main shopping area on the south side. There were nine boys, Mrs. Washington and Kay on the bus. Kay wanted to look around for a place to park the bus but Emily told her to park in front. "That's a bus stop." She said, pointing to the sign. "And this is a bus. Besides no body gonna bother us no how."

Kay had to admit this was one confident lady. They weren't exactly inconspicuous. The boys stood there on the street corner gawking at the buildings as though they were looking at the Statue of Liberty from Ellis Island. Their first taste of freedom in America. Then they got a real taste of America. A shopping spree! They were allowed to pick out all of their own clothes.

Kay and Emily had a great time themselves watching the kids' energy and exuberance. The sales personnel smelled a huge bill and were running around behind the boys with shoe horns, tape measures flying.

After they were finished Mrs. Washington put her huge purse up onto the checkout counter. It thudded when she set it down, Kay suspected she had a pistol in the bottom. When she opened the bag it seemed to be practically full of money. She pulled a handful of bills out and handed them to the smiling clerk.

The boys had insisted on putting their new clothes on immediately, the clothes that the Washington's had given them were reverently folded, then placed in shopping bags by the happy clerks. When they got out on the street Kay felt even more conspicuous.

The boys had chosen loud wild colors, plaids, stripes, paisley prints. One boy was wearing red satin slippers that he must have gotten from the women's shoe department. Standing all together on the corner of 63rd and Halstead they looked like the Jackson Five, times two.

Chapter 66: The Seminary, the Rescue

Curtin left Kelly holding the horses. Kelly would have gone in with them if Curtin wanted him, but this was breaking and entering, plain and simple, Curtin didn't want to take a chance on getting Kelly in any trouble that they couldn't get him out of.

Not only were they not in Chicago, they were in DuPage County, at midnight. There were not a lot of Chicago Police friendly people around here, especially the local law enforcement. Chicago Police had a reputation for brutality, graft and corruption, not undeserved.

Curtin, on the other hand, liked breaking and entering. It was one of his favorite things plus he didn't give a shit about anything, but his objective. He was wound that way. After Kelly moved the car a safe distance away and their eyes adjusted to the darkness, using a rope ladder tossed over the top spikes, Curtin and Dr. Nguyen went over the fence. Nguyen had turned out to be a key player, apparently having skills that never stopped emerging.

Nguyen led the way across the huge lawn keeping to the overgrown tree line. There were no security guards. They had scouted the area right after leaving that afternoon in the daylight and had taken their time checking out the premises and surrounding area tonight. They hadn't seen one police car. When you had a relatively crime free city, the police budget was the first thing that was cut.

Nguyen brought them to an old wooden side door that had a cylinder lock, Curtin had it open in ten seconds. They walked into a kitchen, both carrying penlights with muffled lenses. Nguyen had drawn a schematic of the house from memory after just walking around it during the few minutes he was looking for the boys, they moved toward where they knew there was a servant's staircase.

When Nguyen had found the boys working in the kitchen he learned that there were four boys that needed to be extracted. He didn't think twice about it. He wasn't taking two and leaving two. Then when the original plan had failed, he snapped right to Curtin's Plan B instructing the boys to be ready to leave after midnight.

Nguyen told the boys that the priest he was with was there to rescue them but they were skeptical. They were afraid of men with robes. Nguyen had to tell them that Curtin had killed the priest and taken the beads and robe from him. Coming from a country that was always at war, they understood that. They said they would be ready.

When they made their way up a servant's staircase to the little rooms where the boys slept, they ran into a problem. There were only three boys. Father Adolphus had come and taken one of the boys to his room. Father Adolphus had a room at the front of the house. One of the boys pointed to the door when Nguyen whispered in his ear.

Curtin had signaled to Nguyen that he should wait at the top of the stairs while Curtin got the other boy. And be ready to leave with the boys they already had should something go wrong.

Curtin went to the door the boy had indicated, listening. A man was speaking softly, but he couldn't hear the words because the old wooden door was so thick. Curtin gently grasped the fancy brass knob, it turned.

Curtin pushed the door open forcefully intending to startle the priest, and he did. The man was naked, he turned with a surprised look on his face. Curtin stepped in close and popped the naked man's head back with an uppercut that they used to call 'the Joe Louis Shot' at the gym where he and Kelly had trained for the Golden Gloves as kids. Father Adolphus was unconscious before he hit the deck with a loud thud.

Suddenly Nguyen was at the door, against orders, to back him up. What could Curtin say? They looked to the bed where the little Vietnamese boy was holding a sheet up to his neck like a damsel in distress. Without a word, Nguyen ran in, swept up the boy, sheet and all, and flew out the door like a spirit. Curtin watched him go, knowing that those boys were safe with Nguyen. Then he looked down at the priest.

Curtin closed the door and put the man in the bed. He went into the private bathroom to look for supplies. He found just what he needed. The priest shaved the old fashion way, not with a safety razor and a can that squirts foam. He had a cup with a soft bristle brush, lavender scented soap and an old fashion straight razor. When Curtin had popped him on the button he could tell that he had rung the guy's bell good and that the priest would be out for 10 to 15 minutes at least. Plenty of time.

Curtin was wearing surgical gloves, but had no difficulty

opening the razor and putting it in the priest's right hand. Then, holding the hand with the razor clenched tightly, Curtin guided it up under the man's left arm, into his arm pit pulling it back sharply, straight across, deep into the soft tissue under there, cutting the artery cleanly.

Curtin watched the bastard bleed out for a few moments regretting he had given him such an easy exit. He left without notice, sorry that the Abbott hadn't awakened. He was getting into this Grand Inquisitor thing. Judge, jury, and executioner. Doing God's work.

Chapter 67: The Cardinal's Mansion

"Calm down Father, I can't understand what you're talking about." The man was angry and crying at the same time. Halloran had ensconced himself in the Cardinal's mansion. He had his own suite with an office attached. He had buried Father Francis in the coal bin, locked up the Home and told the answering service to forward his calls to the mansion. As far as he was concerned, Brown could stay out of the country for as long as he wanted. He liked being in charge. He would handle things differently.

"What twenty thousand dollars?" He had the Abbott from the Pendican Seminary on the phone, apparently the man had been calling him since dawn. Fortunately he had told the service to hold all calls until 9:00 a.m.

"The twenty thousand dollars that you demanded for those boys!"

"We demanded nothing, Abbott. Father Brown told you that you could see if the boys.............were up to the standards of the seminary."

"I gave that priest a check for twenty thousand dollars, because he was going to take the boys if I didn't." The Abbott was angrier now that the subject was money.

"What priest?" Halloran couldn't figure out who he was talking about. They were out of priests, except for him, although Father Brown had contacted Amsterdam and six

Mendalin priests were being dispatched from different locations to back them up. Brown had decided that they would use Mendalin priests only from now on.

"The Mendalin priest, Father Tomas 'de!" The Abbott was screaming into the phone. "I gave him a check yesterday and this morning I am informed that the boys are missing, all four of them."

He started sobbing. "And on top of that Father Adolphus has committed suicide during the night. Terrible, this is terrible. Where's my twenty thousand dollars Halloran?" He was screaming again. The thought of losing the money much more painful than losing Father Adolphus.

"Tomas 'de? Are you telling me that a Mendalin priest calling himself Tomas 'de came to the seminary, demanded money and then took the boys we had sent you?" Halloran wasn't so happy to be in charge at the moment. He looked at the person who was on the other side of the desk and thought about asking him to leave, but he had already heard too much. Maybe he could be of help, for a change.

"That's exactly what I'm telling you. A Mendalin priest. Who else could it be? He had the Stigmata on his hands. He said he was acting for Father Brown who is out of the country. Didn't you say that Brown is out of the country? Who is this Father Tomas 'de? What kind of priests are you ordaining?"

"He's not a priest." Halloran was debating how much he should tell the Abbott. He decided as little as possible. "Someone has impersonated one of our order. We don't know who it is, but we have the Chief Investigator of the Archdiocese working on it personally. He looked across his desk and Sanguini smiled at him, nodding agreement. Then he had another thought.

"Abbott, you said that Father Adolphus committed suicide last night?"

"Sadly, yes."

"Is he still there at the seminary?"

"No, I couldn't stand to have a dead body here in the building. The police said we could move him and I had the people from St. Casimir's pick him up to prepare him for burial."

"We're so sorry for your loss Abbott. As for the money you lost, I am going to send you a check to cover the twenty thousand dollars that you were apparently swindled out of. And concerning the other two boys, you will get the money you paid for them back as well. Father Brown is overseas right now but I'm sure he will give you first pick of the new shipment of......uh........orphans, when they are brought over from Vietnam."

That pleased the Abbott and Halloran felt he had hung onto an important client, then he had another thought. "Abbott, we'd like to also pay all the expenses for the funeral and internment of Father Adolphus as a token of our deepest sympathies. Could you give me the contact information on the people who are caring for Father Adolphus?"

After he hung up he looked over at Sanguini, who had been summoned to his office for a dressing down on his lack of progress on finding the missing boys. Now, he had to ask the greasy bastard for a favor. But he was still in charge.

"Sanguini. You better have something for me goddammit or you're going out that fucking window." They were on the third floor, but the look on Halloran's face told Sanguini that he wasn't kidding.

Sanguini wasn't scared though. All he cared about was money and these crazy priests had it by the bushel. He offered that guy twenty grand just to keep him quiet. Sanguini would have quieted him permanently for half that.

"Tell you what, Father, I've got a name, but it cost me plenty to get it. You understand?"

Halloran was still thinking about tossing him out the window. "Tell me the name and I'll tell you what it's worth."

"Curtin. He's a pal of Kelly's." Sanguini smiled like a pirate.

Sanguini knew he had hit a home run, Halloran suddenly figured out exactly who was running this whole operation, that *cop* who had come to the Home impersonating an Internal Affairs investigator. Said his name was Durkin.

He was apparently impersonating other people as well. After settling on a price for just the name, Halloran told Sanguini to spare no expense finding the people behind all of this, starting with Curtin.

After the investigator left, Halloran called the funeral home where they had taken Father Adolphus. He made arrangements to keep his promise to pay for the funeral, then he asked to speak to the person who was actually preparing the corpse. A man named Phil came to the phone.

The guy started talking immediately saying, "Yes Father. I'm taking care of Father Adolphus, you bet, very good. You bet. No one's gonna see that he.......you know.......killed his self."

"Fine." Halloran had no patience for fools. "Phil, was it? Can you tell me if there was anything written on Father Adolphus?"

"No. I mean, not really Father. He didn't write no suicide note on his self, if that's what you is askin. But he did maybe write something on his hand, the palm of his left hand, a word maybe. I saw it when I was washin him you know, real reverent like."

"A word?" Halloran asked. "What was the word?"

"Well, I was busy washin him up you see, I couldn't really tell 'cause I washed it some before I noticed..."

"What was the word man?" Halloran yelled into the phone.

Startled into silence for a moment, the man went on cautiously. "Well, it was washed off some....but it looked like *Tornado*. You know we had some bad storms here the other day, maybe he was trying to remember there was going to be a tornado."

Halloran hung up. He hoped Sanguini would eliminate this Torquemada maniac quickly, he was paying him enough, but he would surely love to have his hands around the bastard's neck at the moment, considering all the trouble he had caused. He didn't know the half of it.

Chapter 68: Curtin's Kitchen

Twenty thousand bucks is twice as much money than I make in a year. It didn't look like much, just two tiny little stacks, but I was glad to get rid of it. Curtin had handed it to me in the bank when we cashed the Abbott's check. The bank was closing but Curtin wasn't waiting until tomorrow. He wasn't waiting another minute.

He told the bank Vice President, who had been summoned by the clerk Curtin was berating, that the check was drawn on his bank, that he didn't need an account to cash it and that if he didn't have his money in five minutes, he would have the Archdiocese of Chicago cease doing business with his bank and any of its affiliates. The banker called the Abbott to see if the check was good, after that we had the money in four minutes.

I put the money on the table. Sitting around the Curtin's kitchen table were Liz, Michael, Curtin and me. Dr. Nguyen was also there, obviously part of the family now.

"So, not only did we get the kids, we got twenty grand to help offset their expenses. Not bad for a day's, work." Curtin smiled at Michael and Liz, she didn't smile back.

"What?" Curtin asked her. "How did you do?"

"I did better than you." Liz said. She had a legal pad in front of her covered with figures.

"How much better?" Curtin pushed the cash across the table as though he was making a raise in a card game. She ignored the move and looked at her figures. We had a little sibling rivalry going here.

"Well, if I take your twenty thousand off of the figure I have, I still beat you by.....uh.....eight hundred seventy eight thousand, four hundred eleven dollars and sixty seven cents."

Curtin smiled, clearly whipped by his big sister. "Sixty seven cents? Are you sure of that?"

She ignored his quip. "And I have it working for the boys in a number of ways already, starting with a money market account earning 9% interest."

Nobody was making fun of those kinds of results. She added, "With thanks to Mr. Nguyen, who is a financial genius, if you ask me." No one was asking her anything.

"Mr. Nguyen showed me how to use the information we already had to uncover additional accounts that the priests had in their names. Brown, Halloran, and a couple of others donated three hundred thou all by themselves. Bless their hearts."

She smiled at the little man with the multiple talents. "My favorite idea was a soccer club. Now, the boys are all members of the Saigon Soccer Club, a non-profit organization. The money has been moved from one bank to another until it was finally moved to one of our banks. They will never be able to find it."

One of *our* banks meant it was controlled by her husband

and they had more rules than the government regarding disclosure of customer information, and their penalties were a lot more severe than the government's punishments. So, it seemed that the kids would have money for future needs. There were thirteen now.

The homecoming at Mr. Washington's house had been joyous. It turned out that the boys were all from the same province. They were *purchased* from an unscrupulous orphanage director in Saigon by Father Brown, then shipped to America in twos and threes over the past year.

The boys remembered the silver haired Father Brown, with his beads around his waist, picking them out as though they were livestock, making them walk up and down, open their mouths for him to check their teeth. The youngest ones were ignored, the older ones too. There were girls chosen in the same way, but the boys never saw any of them again after they were chosen.

Chapter 69: The Cardinal's Mansion

"My check bounced! What's going on back there?" Brown was screaming into the phone from Hawaii so loudly it sounded like he was in the room, which Halloran was extremely grateful he was not.

Halloran had just found out that the bank accounts had been emptied. Sanguini had come storming in waving the check he had given him with an ISF stamp on it, he had been forced to give the greasy bastard all of the cash he had with him, five thousand dollars. Worse yet, he had sent the Abbott a bad check. Besides murdering everyone this damn Torquemada bastard was ruining his life.

The Vice President at Drover's Bank took Halloran's frantic call saying that Father Francis had come in with a nun and made her a signatory on the accounts. They had indicated that they were doing some special missionary work, and by the end of the day all of the funds had been moved. Halloran was screaming into the phone that there had to be some mistake.

The Vice President tried to explain that he had spoken with the clerks who had checked the signature cards, also matching Father Francis' signature with his driver's license which he presented.

Father Francis also presented proxy forms signed by Fathers' Brown and Halloran that had verified the transfers from their personal accounts. All of the signatures on the transfer forms had been witnessed by Father Brown. The only problem was that Father Francis was buried in the basement, but he couldn't very well tell them that.

"It must be the man Sanguini told us about, Curtin. From the descriptions it seems that he's the one that's running around dressed like a Mendalin. He's good at these deceptions, the Abbott said he had the scars of the Stigmata on his hands. He must have gotten the banking information when he was at the house torturing Francis to death." He crossed himself.

"I'm sending you six Mendalin's. Go to the weapons warehouse and draw Mach 10's for them with suppressors and enough ammo...... a lot of ammo, get anything you think you might need. Do you understand?" Brown was still fuming.

"And get this banking shit straightened out. Call Geneva and have a couple of hundred thousand transferred stateside. Not to Drover's Bank. Send the Abbott forty with our apologies and assure him that he will have first pick of the new boys when we bring them over. And make sure the accounts are secure, no adding names. Do you think you can do that without screwing up?"

He had already done that, but Halloran kept his mouth shut, hoping Brown would choke on the Mai Tai he was probably sipping by the pool.

"Until the Mendalin's get there, get our monies worth out of that asshole of Cardinal Sloane's." He didn't have to worry on that account, Halloran had given Sanguini his personal money. He wasn't going to see that again, Brown would be checking the books personally from now on, he knew.

However two hundred grand would give him enough working capital to have Sanguini put more personnel on tracking Curtin, Kelly, and anybody else that had been involved in stealing his money. That was all Halloran cared about, Curtin had stolen from the wrong person.

Father Brown was calculating, "Considering that Paul, Julian, and that asshole Goddard are all missing, probably incinerated in the crematory, we have to proceed as though those boys are alive."

Halloran had come to that conclusion when he had toured the burned out building with the Fire Marshall. Someone, probably Curtin or Kelly, had turned both furnaces to maximum, then left the doors to the crematories open. The fire that destroyed the building was so hot the metal beams melted like wax.

"Counting the four boys that they kidnapped from the seminary they have thirteen now. How the hell can they hide thirteen Vietnamese boys? They've got to be somewhere. Find out where they are hiding them. Then kill them all. Do you understand? I want a goddamn blood bath, no witnesses, no Curtin, no Kelly, also anyone who's with them, or knows anything about this whole matter."

Halloran figured Brown was foaming at the mouth by now. Brown wanted him to kill half of Chicago. Even Al Capone didn't kill as many people as Father Brown wanted him to kill. Maybe he could take the two hundred grand, go to a place somewhere in the world where Brown couldn't find him.

"I'd like to stake Kelly and Curtin onto a bamboo sprout, God curse them!" Halloran shivered. He remembered all too well Brown's favorite torture when they were in the jungle. Sit a man on top of a newly sprouted bamboo tip and stake him down. A bamboo sprout could grow twelve inches or more in a day. Sometimes the man would live a couple of days, screaming constantly. Halloran could still hear the screaming sometimes at night.

"Yes Father. I'll do exactly what you want." That was the only answer he had for a man like Father Antonin Brown. Halloran made the sign of the cross again, more sincerely this time, if there was such a thing.

Chapter 70: Juvenile Court

Things quieted down after a few days and started to return to a semblance of normalcy. I was doing my regular job, writing up kids for stealing cars or smoking pot, then releasing them to their mothers. I had court coming up with Franklin Palmer so I prepared my court documents for the next day.

Kay quit her job at the Audy Home, she was now the official team nurse and driver for the Saigon Soccer Club. Liz fixed it up, Kay was happy, so who was I to question, we could always get the job back for her if she wanted it. The only problem was that now I couldn't get Kay to go out with me because she was constantly working with the boys. At least that was how it seemed. There was always something, now they all had colds and Mrs. Washington was making chicken soup in gigantic pots like we used to use in the army mess hall.

The Juvenile Court in Chicago served the entire city, which was why it was immense. Early in the morning I wandered the halls until I figured out I was on the wrong floor, my hearing room was downstairs. When I walked in Franklin was already there flanked by two Cook County Sheriff's Deputies. Lorna Franklin was also there, I sat next to her instead of in the policemen's row in front.

By the time our case was called, I had already talked to the State's Attorney, Franklin was remanded to the custody of the Juvenile Court until he was twenty-one years old or was deemed rehabilitated enough to be released. He would be receiving counseling, going to school. He would be re-examined by doctors regularly to assess his progress. Lorna Franklin could hardly contain her gratitude. I was hoping the doctors and counselors could make a difference in Franklin's life so that he didn't hit the streets in six years ready to kill again.

As I left the courtroom, I saw Frankie Bartuca in the hallway. "What's up?" I asked him.

"I'm here on that kidnapping case, you know Barbara Cunningham?" The way he said it made me ask another question, she was an adult so I knew she couldn't be going to court in the Juvenile Court house.

"So what are you doing in Juvenile Court?"

"You won't believe it. The mother of the kidnapped baby is a heroin addict, the baby was born with heroin in his bloodstream, now they're taking the baby away from her, giving it up for adoption."

Sad, but that was the way it went in our twisted judicial system. Women who were addicts lost their children just because of that fact. It didn't matter what else was going on in their lives. If the baby tested positive, the State took the baby. And just try to get the kid back, it was impossible.

"That's too bad, but that's the State's method for punishing female drug addicts." I smelled more to the story. "So what is there about it that I won't believe?"

"They're giving the kid to Barbara Cunningham." He said

with a little crooked smile on his face, knowing how I would react.

"What! They're giving the kid to the woman who kidnapped him? Are they out of their minds?"

"No, they're giving the kid to her husband, though they're not legally married, they have a common law marriage." I couldn't believe that either.

Just then two people came out of the courtroom we were standing in front of. One was Clarence Turner in his Peoples Gas Company uniform, the other was Terry Bloom the vulture. Now I knew why they were giving the baby to the kidnapper. Money.

Turner recognized me, but pretended he hadn't, quickly looking away. I knew why, the fix was going in, he didn't want me around, I had already screwed up his life enough.

Terry Bloom was a notorious Family Court attorney. These bottom feeder attorneys were so incompetent that they couldn't support themselves in private practice, so they hung around the Family Court rooms selling children when they could get their dirty hands on them. Otherwise, these court house leeches survived on the crumbs that they were paid to represent indigent clients when they were appointed by the court to represent someone.

They knew how to spread the grease around when they had a paying client though, everybody was in for a piece of the pie from the judge on down to the bailiff. I looked at her as she consulted with her client, dollar signs glinting in her eyes.

The rest of her looked like a person who had given up on life a long time ago. She was grossly overweight. Her hair was uncombed, clothing stained from food that hadn't made it to her mouth over the past few days. She was as dangerous as a rattle snake.

Clarence Turner was a middle class citizen who worked hard for a living. Bloom would happily take him for every dime he had. She would get him to sign a promissory note to cover her fees, then garnish his wages until the day he died.

Bartuca told me that the deal had already been done, that they were just phonying up the documents. They made Clarence Turner the baby's legal 'godfather' by statute definition so he could adopt. To back it up they had a document from the baby's mother giving Turner 'Directed Consent' to adopt her child. Bartuca said they had threatened the mother with jail if she didn't sign, another kick in the gut to a woman who had carried this child for nine months.

Frankie also guessed, I agreed, that none of this would be happening regardless of how much money he spread around if the new father didn't have some heavy political clout. In Chicago black people voted, therefore, they had clout if they knew the right people. Once he adopted the baby, Turner would use that clout to open up other doors, cell doors.

When the wife's case came up in criminal court the word would travel with her case that there were favors, and money, being exchanged here. The State's Attorneys would go along. Everybody went along when it came down to money and power. Justice and injustice were commodities in Chicago, just like human beings.

Chapter 71: Kelly's House

Curtin was always paranoid, more so these days. Although things were quiet he never relaxed his vigilance which paid off when he noticed he was being followed by some pretty talented people. They were using three cars, they weren't crowding him, very professional.

Tailing someone in a big city like Chicago is difficult, because there are so many stop lights. You often had to blow red lights if you wanted to maintain the tail. That presented a number of problems, you could be noticed by the person you were tailing, get stopped by a cop, or more likely get T-boned in an intersection. Using three cars reduced those problems significantly.

Their only problem was that they were tailing the master. Making it look accidental, Curtin made a quick turn into a White Castle losing them easily. He then circled back, picked up one of the cars, following him back to his office, which was Paramount Investigations, way up on Higgins Road on the North Side. Now the new question was who would hire private detectives to follow him. There were only a few possibilities.

Regardless, Curtin had a problem. He couldn't kill these people. They were regular people who were doing a job they were hired for. They weren't an international crime ring of pedophiles that couldn't let themselves be found out. He would have to think of something creative that would send several messages at the same time.

His second favorite job was cab driver. He went over to the taxi maintenance lot on 23rd and Wabash. After a brief conversation with an old friend and a green handshake, he drove out of the lot in a Yellow Cab, vacancy light on top, meter, number on the side, everything. He even had a cap with an emblem on it. He liked hats.

Sure it was hard to tail people in Chicago, but not if you were essentially invisible. There were thousands of Yellow Cabs on the streets. Because they were everywhere you looked, nobody noticed taxi cabs unless they needed one.

Curtin followed the team from Paramount and soon realized they were tagging Kelly too. He'd have to warn Kelly, again, to stay away from the Washington's. What he wanted to know was who had hired the detective agency and why. So he decided to bug their cars, they had two way radios in their cars, Curtin was going to make them three way radios.

Down in his lab he constructed bugs that also had some extra features that could be operated remotely. He had been one of the first people to buy a television with a remote control, he had been fascinated with them ever since. After he put the bugs in the cars they would broadcast all the time. All he had to do was listen and he would hopefully find out who was onto them. It had to be the priests, but he needed more details.

They were using two cars with four men on Kelly, sparing no expense. They were sitting where they could watch his house from different angles. They were just watching though, they weren't a hit team, Curtin could tell.

One team had unwittingly parked over the burned pavement where there had been a car/truck fire recently. That brought a cynical smile to Curtin's face, those bastards that he burned in that car were going to assassinate Kelly. They deserved what they got. These men however had only to be persuaded to go into another line of work.

Kelly was sitting at home now after receiving a call from Curtin telling him about the surveillance. Kelly wasn't happy about not being able to go near the Washington's or about not seeing Kay Miller. He also wasn't happy about being the bait for this plan.

Curtin was parked near enough to one of the teams to clearly listen in on their conversation over his FM radio. He had ditched the other teams that had tried to follow him when he left his house.

Allright was keeping an eye on them though, Curtin had given him the cab. He was having a great time playing undercover cab driver. Curtin suspected him of picking up some fares, but didn't care as long as he was on the private detectives' asses while doing it. Probably made him look more legitimate.

"I still don't like this whole set-up," the one with the deeper voice said.

"Me neither, but double pay is double pay." Curtin turned up the volume.

"They're only giving us more money to keep our mouths shut. And probably because we're likely to get shot tailing two cops."

"I agree with you on that. I don't like messing with Chicago PD. They fuckin shoot you and after you're dead they make it look like you were the bad guy."

"And if anything happens, don't expect to get any back up from our client. We're out on a limb here Sam."

"Yea, I don't like that greaser one bit. First thing he says is that he's an ex-homicide dick. Like that means shit to us. Everybody used to be on the job before they start working as a PI, they expect it to be on the resume."

"I heard he got that job with the Archdiocese after he caught some big shot Monsignor diddling a little boy in the back seat of his car. Now, he's their Chief Investigator. Lucky bastard."

Curtin had heard enough. He pushed the button on a TV remote control, valves opened in the two tail cars. Odorless gas hissed into the vehicles. He hoped it didn't kill them, he had been guaranteed that it wouldn't, but the government had been wrong before about their experimental weapons.

Chapter 72: The Cardinal's Mansion

"What the hell are you talking about?" Halloran was tired of this dago barging in on him. He was waiting for a call from the bank in Zurich, so he could have more money transferred. He had taken the cheat sheet with the account numbers out of his wallet, he covered it with his hand.

Brown made him memorize the numbers, but he had made a copy in case he forgot. He wanted to get the account numbers right when they called and asked for them. He needed more money, quickly. He had people coming at him from every direction with their hands out.

There were a million things to do, cancel and arrange. The insurance adjuster had been to the warehouse and it actually looked like they were going to make a killing from the insurance claim. If they had been able to find any traces of Julian or Paul, they might have gotten more.

"Here, read it for yourself." Sanguini handed him a sheet of parchment paper with hand written calligraphic lettering.

> *"You are marked for death. You live now only by the slightest chance that you do not know who you are working for. The Grand Inquisitor Torquemada has condemned the priests of Mendalin to be wiped from the earth for their evil deeds. The ones who hire you are their agents. They will be destroyed also. Do not waver in the belief that I will reach out for you if*

Halloran finished reading the note. Sanguini had a strange look on his face. Halloran couldn't tell if the man was angry or scared. Sanguini pointed at the document.

"That note was found in the cars of the private detectives I hired to watch Curtin and Kelly. They were somehow knocked out, when they woke up the note was on the dash board, both cars, four men."

"Sounds like they scare pretty easily." Halloran tossed the note down on the desk.

"They're scared shitless." He picked it up. "You read this line about looking into your palm? He branded them all."

"What are you talking about?"

"Branded. What the hell did you do to this guy? He heated up a crucifix and burned the thing into the palms of their hands. The story is all over the city, I couldn't get guys to work for me now if I paid them ten times what I gave the guys from Paramount."

Just then there was a knock on the door to Halloran's suite. Happy for the interruption he called out for the person to come in. The door opened and a little Mendalin priest came into the room, approached the desk and introduced himself to Halloran, ignoring Sanguini.

"Father Halloran? I am Orlando. I am at your service."

Halloran turned to Sanguini, telling him that his services would no longer be needed, that he would also not be paid anything further. Sanguini left without any argument, Father Orlando had that effect on people.

Chapter 73: Jackson Park

Now that he thought he had some breathing room, Curtin went looking for Tombs, real name Antomee Callwell. He had an address that was a phony and an old mug shot that probably looked nothing like the guy. Allright knew him but not where he lived. All Curtin knew was that he dressed flashy and wore his hair in a huge Afro. That narrowed it down to eighty percent of the men.

Curtin had a bad feeling about the conversation he had with Allright when he was inquiring about the triple homicide on the south side. Curtin didn't really care how many people Tombs killed, it was the mention of a new type of weapon. Curtin had a machine gun in his possession now also, a gun that had created a lot of questions that had no answers, as yet. Curtin had to know if the one Tombs had was a match to his, it would link Tombs to the Mendalins.

Gang bangers shooting each other was one thing, but black militant groups armed with machine guns could mean a blood bath someplace where a lot of innocent people would be killed. They would be innocent white people probably, which couldn't be a worse thing for black people as a whole.

Curtin's problem was how to find Tombs. The only way to get a junkie to talk was to bribe him, not with money, the only thing that junkies were interested in was heroin. So he acquired a quantity of heroin, about twenty balloons, which would sell on the street for a hundred each. He picked out a bench in Jackson Park, sat down, and waited for a junkie to come by.

He figured Tombs would find out pretty quickly that there was a white guy in the park giving away heroin and asking questions about him. The plan was a little crazy but he thought it was worth a try. He didn't have to wait long. The first junkie he tried to give a balloon to, was an undercover cop. So much for that idea.

"You are under arrest! Man I ought to work you over, coming down here with that bullshit."

"No, I'm not. Don't be dramatic." Curtin was in the back seat of a Chevy Nova that was an undercover vice car. He looked like he was under arrest though, especially with the handcuffs he was wearing behind his back.

"I know who you are," the driver said, dismissing his partner's hysterics after Curtin had identified himself. "Don't mean shit in our park man. As far as we know you're a bad cop, selling a little H on the side."

The partner that wanted to arrest Curtin was a tall thin black guy with a big afro. He was dressed in raggedy clothes and fit the junkie profile perfectly. He even had tattooed track marks in the pit of his left elbow.

The driver had a better idea. "You're thinking that you can come into our territory and do any goddamn thing you want because you're heavy. Well, you're carrying two grand worth of China White and you got no back-up so you're flying solo. We'll let you call your Chinaman when we get to the station, but it's gonna cost you and him. Understand? Curtin." He made sure he said the name so there would be no mistake.

"I still say we ought to lock this mother fucker up and

run the paperwork through. He says he's lookin for Tombs. Why don't he come to us? Cause he's making money in our territory." The fake junkie looked back at Curtin. "Go back the fuck up to the white neighborhood, man."

That gave Curtin an idea. "If you want to lock me up, fine, but I am asking you, very nicely, to let me talk to your commander, before, during or after you do that." That was all he said. They knew better than to refuse, they'd end up getting it from both ends. There was no *nicely* on this job.

Chapter 74: Area 3 Vice Control Division

Curtin sat in Lieutenant Parelli's office on the second floor of the 3rd Area Police Detective's building. The Youth Office where Kelly worked was at the other end of the hall. After a lot of accusations and threats were made, Parelli finally agreed to make a few phone calls and he and Curtin were buddies now. The two undercover junkies were sent back to Needle Park.

"Explain it to me again, Tom." Parelli said. They were on a first name basis now, a one way first name basis.

"Well, Lieutenant, this Tombs character is more than your average drug dealer. I believe he has access to new weapons technology. He's supposed to have used a machine gun that no one has ever seen before." Curtin couldn't tell the Lieutenant that he actually had one of these weapons in his possession and that his brother Danny had picked up at the Graves Registration building while they were rescuing the boys, just before the building mysteriously burned to the ground.

Curtin had checked it out through his sources in the government. The machine gun was made by Military Armaments Corporation, it was a Model 10. Invented by Gordon B. Ingram in 1964. Commonly known as the MAC 10. The weapon fired .45 caliber ammunition at a rate of 1250 rounds per minute. You could cut a building in half with just one. These weapons were only accessible by special military units, not regular Army and by no means civilians.

"How do we know that?" Parelli was in no hurry to get involved in any games. Pretty smart, considering who was pitching.

"That's privileged information sir, but rest assured, it is accurate. My informant told me that Tombs mowed those three gang bangers down like wheat. If we could find that gun or better yet find out where he got that gun, it would be a big feather in your cap."

Curtin leaned in closer from where he was sitting next to the Lieutenant's desk, lowering his voice conspiratorially, "And of course, my Division would not want to be on the paper." That clinched it. Parelli ordered everybody to start looking for Tombs.

As it turned out Harrigan and Weathers, the two guys who had nabbed Curtin in the first place, had found Tombs and were already heading back into the station with him from their junkie haven in Jackson Park, hoping that this would get them off the dime. It did.

When they brought Tombs in Curtin looked at him thinking he wouldn't have been too hard to find. Tombs wasn't exactly inconspicuous. His afro was as wide as his shoulders and he was wearing an orange polyester suit with a frilly purple shirt, walking unsteadily on stacked white leather boots. The vice guys made it clear that Tombs was their pinch and that Curtin was only a bystander.

Curtin hung back and let them take the reins. Parelli knew what was coming and decided that his shift was over and announced he could be reached at home. He wanted to have a distance of plausible deniability between himself and this interrogation.

They started out brother to brother, telling Tombs that they would take care of him. They knew he had committed the triple murders but they understood that it was a family honor thing, the jury would certainly see that, all he had to do was tell them about the machine gun, being brothers they promised to take good care of him. Tombs called them all 'Pigs' and spit on a couple of guys, that's when the brother to brother stuff ended.

Four guys took turns on Tombs. They worked him over pretty good, when that didn't loosen his tongue they threatened to charge him with the heroin they had taken off of Curtin. Then, they told him he was going down for the triple homicide and the murder of Johnny Slater, too. That was a new one for Curtin, but he didn't mind. He needed to find out about the gun. Curtin waited for them to get tired and asked if he could have a shot at Tombs.

"I ain't letting you beat up no brother, man." Weathers said.

Curtin smiled. "You guys have been beating him for hours and he's laughing at you. I don't think beating him is the answer."

Weathers had a twisted sense of right and wrong. It was apparently okay for him to beat up 'a brother' but he didn't want Curtin doing it. When they hesitated Curtin told the four of them to take a hike or he'd call Parelli up at home. That worked like a charm, Curtin didn't know Parelli personally, but the fear he struck in his men spoke volumes.

The interrogation room was small, painted puke green, it was used to hold prisoners while processing. Metal rings were set into the back wall at intervals over a wooden bench that ran from one side of the room to the other. There was a large table in the center with unmatched chairs around it, there were two large windows with wooden sashes pushed up leaving the bottom parts open to the night air.

Tombs was handcuffed to a wooden armchair. His afro was on sideways now and he was bleeding from a cut over his eye that was swelling shut. His orange suit was splattered with blood, it didn't match. Curtin hated amateurs, these vice guys were the worst. Striking someone in the face created a lot of damage that just looked bad, but didn't hurt that much, considering you were trying to inflict enough pain to make someone tell you things they refused to reveal.

Once you started beating someone it became a contest, it encouraged them to resist even more. The trick was that you had to make the subject believe that there were worse things to come. Curtin entered the interrogation room, went over to where Tombs was sitting and looked down at him. Tombs looked up and smiled. There was blood in his mouth.

Curtin wasn't a big guy but he was built like a fire plug. Without saying a word he bent over and picked Tombs up, chair, handcuffs and all, and threw him out the window.

"AAAAaaaaaaa.........." The scream faded away as Tombs plummeted towards the ground. Curtin turned and walked out of the room.

"He escaped." Curtin said to the four stunned vice guys as he brushed past them and headed for the stairs.

When he reached the lobby everyone at the desk was looking around trying to figure out where all the screaming was coming from. Curtin didn't even acknowledge them, he headed for the door. He had business out on the street.

Tombs was lying on the pavement under the window he had been launched from, an orange tangle of broken furniture, hair and handcuffs. As Curtin approached him he noted that Tombs was still alive, the chair seeming to have broken his fall.

Curtin reached down and grabbed the handcuffs, Tombs had been wearing two pairs linked together under the now demolished chair, and started dragging Tombs back towards the door. Tombs started to moan and looked up to see Curtin's determined face.

Tombs screamed. "You crazy mother fucker! Throw me out the fuckin window!" He didn't seem any worse for wear, no broken bones apparently, his suit had taken a beating though.

Curtin dragged Tombs up to the door of the station. "Man what the fuck are you doin?" Tombs screamed, obviously in pain.

"You don't tell me about that gun, you're going out again." Curtin said matter-of-factly, and started dragging him up the stairs. Tombs really started screaming now.

"No.....No......I'll tell you! Don't throw me out the window again man! No....Please...I'll tellllllll...."

Chapter 75: Curtin's Kitchen

When Curtin called me and told me we were going on a raid, I held my breath until he told me it was a real raid, with real cops and a search warrant. What a relief. When will I learn?

My first surprise was a real Army Captain sitting at the table in the Curtin's kitchen. His hat had its own chair. While sipping coffee and finishing a piece of Danish, the man was chatting with Mrs. Curtin about Notre Dame's chances of winning it all this year. Notre Dame was her favorite topic. The guy knew how to charm a lady.

Ray O'Connell was commander of Army Intelligence stationed at Fort Sheridan, up north on Lake Michigan. After I was introduced, Curtin told me there had been a little change in plan. We were going to stiff the vice guys on the pinch. I was betting that would make us lots of new friends, angry ones with guns.

"Let me get that thing for you, Ray," Curtin said and went down to the laboratory while we said goodbye to Mrs. Curtin. Captain O'Connell laid the Irish blarney on thick. He had her grinning from ear to ear.

When we met outside, three green Military Police vehicles had appeared at the curb. I knew we wouldn't be taking my car, Curtin hated my Camaro, but I didn't think the Army would be providing the transportation. I was riding shotgun, Curtin and O'Connell were in the back. Curtin had a brown paper bag, opening it he took out a wicked looking weapon. It had a short barrel only about twenty inches long overall. It also had a long magazine that held who knows how many rounds.

"That's it!" Taking the weapon from Curtin, O'Connell racked the action, checking the chamber in a knowledgeable way, while pointing the barrel in a safe direction. "How the hell they got their hands on this weapon amazes me. I checked the serial number you gave me, it doesn't even exist."

"Well, I don't think it's the only one that doesn't exist," Curtin said.

"They must have a person with a lot of contacts in Special Forces, ordinance and armament manufacturers. That's a long list." He looked over at Curtin. "You didn't tell me where you got this weapon Tom, I won't press you, but I would appreciate it if you could give me a little something to go on. A name, anything."

"Ever hear of a Master Sergeant named Terrance Goddard?" Curtin asked.

"Son of a bitch! That guy is on our radar. He's working here in Chicago in Graves Registration. We had word that he was involved in some kind of smuggling. I'll have him picked up right away."

"Tell them to bring a dust pan and a broom," Curtin said, and just looked at O'Connell. We didn't talk for the rest of the trip out to the Airport.

Chapter 76: The Home

There were seven determined men around the large table in the dining room. Mail bags were stacked to the ceiling against one wall. They were drinking Oolong Tea, strange choice for men who were Special Forces operatives from four different countries that had completed missions in the most dangerous war zones around the world.

They were also priests. The Mendalin Missionary's considered themselves Crusaders, Knights Templar. They not only considered themselves above the laws of man, but also above the laws of the Catholic Church. They privately called themselves the Angels of Death.

These men had been personally recruited by Father Brown, who had shown them the way to the Light without sacrificing the principles that they all held. The Catholic Church was in a war against evil forces that were trying to destroy it. It could only be victorious by eliminating these enemies.

Chief among these enemies were; the Islamists, Jews and Evangelicals, although anyone who was not a Catholic was the enemy in their eyes. The only tenant of the Koran that they admired was that anyone who was not a Muslim was an infidel and must be either converted or destroyed. That made sense to a Mendalin Missionary.

At the head of the table was Father Halloran. He was conducting the meeting, he was in charge of all missions. He was reveling in his roll. To his right was Father Orlando, who had come to the Cardinal's mansion and started the ball rolling, making it possible for him to fire that grease ball, Sanguini.

Orlando was a former Commando from the Philippines, who was such a fanatically devout Catholic that when Father Brown had asked him if he would be willing to suffer the agony of the wounds of Christ to protect the Church, Orlando had pulled out a knife and stabbed it through his hand pinning it to the table they were sitting at. The only one there who didn't have the five wounds of Christ was Orlando. What was the point? Father Brown had thought at the time.

Next to Orlando were Peres and Louis. They were ex-members of the most elite unit of what was commonly known as the French Foreign Legion. After being drummed out of the service for raping and murdering two children, Father Brown found them guarding shipments of opium out of Afghanistan. He converted them to the Mendalin Mission ideals and then sponsored them to the priesthood. They smuggle heroin for God now.

Peres and Louis would gladly lay down their lives for Father Brown, especially after he had absolved them and cleansed their souls of all of their sins, which had shocked even Father Brown when he had heard their confessions.

Hans and Kroner were former Belgium Special Forces Commandos, who had fought in Cambodia and Laos after their French counterparts had fucked up the entire region trying to retain their part of Indo China after WWII. Hans ran the orphanages and smuggled children to clients all over the world. Kroner was the weapons man. He gazed lovingly at what was on the table in front of him.

Last, on Halloran's left hand, was Shaun Regan, who had no special training, but was the person who had more to be forgiven than any of the others combined. He had been an assassin for the Irish Republican Army. Father Brown had broken him out of an English prison and brought him to the Mendalin's. Regan had killed men, women and children indiscriminately, in the name of the Catholic Church. He had a burning desire to kill the enemies of the Church every minute of every day, even when he was saying mass and begging God for forgiveness. He was a diminutive man, but everybody was afraid of him.

Chapter 77: Midway Airport Storage Facility

The warehouse where Tombs told Curtin he had gotten the machine gun wasn't a big building. Tucked into a residential neighborhood it was two stories and about a hundred feet square. There was one pedestrian door in front and a roll up door next to it that could accommodate a large vehicle.

There had been a lot of these buildings built in these neighborhoods to accommodate the shipping going in and out of Midway Airport over the years. Now O'Hare Airport was the focus, Midway, and the area around it, were nearly forgotten. It was very convenient for shipping weapons disguised as farm equipment.

Lieutenant Parelli was there with every man in his unit, day off or not. They had sledge hammers, giant bolt cutters, big flashlights and guns, lots of guns. They had told Curtin that they were going to surround the building and go in at eleven o'clock. He knew they were lying and had the station watched by his brother Danny, who had the day off from the firehouse. Danny called him from the Huckleberry Finn Donut Shop across the street from the station when he saw them loading up their cars.

Curtin figured they would go right after sunset so he planned to just show up after the vice guys secured the area, about seven-thirty. He figured it was a fifty-fifty shot as to whether the priests had people in the warehouse who were armed to the teeth. In that case Parelli and his boys would have had a shootout and the chips would have fallen.

Regardless of who got shot, Curtin knew he would have an easier time of it when he got there with the Army. Too bad if some of the casualties happened to be Parelli's guys, and Curtin had a couple of hopefuls for that honor. Some posthumous medals would be nice for Harrigan and Weathers.

But things were going smoothly, which made Kelly very happy, Curtin not so much. There was apparently no one in the warehouse, considering Parelli and his men had been about as tactful as a herd of elephants setting up the perimeter. They were just busting down the front door with a big two man battering ram when Curtin arrived with the Calvary.

The door went down and six of the Vice men charged into the building each carrying a different kind of weapon. One guy even had a Thompson Sub-machine gun like Capone and his boys used in the twenties. The Military Police officers alighted from their vehicles led by Captain O'Connell and Curtin, followed up by Kelly who was guarding the rear.

The building was unoccupied, which had pissed Lieutenant Parelli off, he turned to Curtin with a bad attitude, that was just about to get a lot worse.

"Curtin, you said that junkie you almost killed told you there was a gang of black militants holed up here ready to start a street war." He was fuming. "Where are the heads you promised me?"

"Lieutenant, if you're talking about the informant I captured when he escaped from your office, that's what he told me. Actually he was ready to confess to assassinating Kennedy, but that's neither here nor there." Curtin waved in the air.

"There's been a change of plans," Curtin pointed to Captain O'Connell.

"Oh yea? Who the hell is this guy and what do you think you're doing at my crime scene." Parelli pointed at O'Connell. "This is our city and my district, we have a search warrant that gives us possession of everything in that building. Even if there are no physical arrests to be made." He sneered at Curtin.

O'Connell got in Parelli's face. To his credit, the Lieutenant stood his ground. "Lieutenant Parelli, my name is Captain Raymond O'Connell. I am Commander of Military Intelligence out of Fort Sheridan and I am in command of this mission. In fact I am in command of the ground that you are standing on."

"Lieutenant Collingsworth." O'Connell spoke over Parelli's shoulder to where his second in command and other MP's had deployed themselves in a tactical pattern to cover every man that Parelli had standing around gawking at the exchange.

"This area is now a Federal Crime Scene." O'Connell waved his hand gesturing towards Parelli's men. "Disarm these men and search each one of them. I want their identification cards confiscated. And if there is any disagreement, I point out that this is considered a matter in which lethal force is authorized."

O'Connell's men pulled their Colt Commander 45's and had the drop on the clueless vice guys in two seconds. Parelli started to protest but O'Connell just brushed past him indicating with his thumb that Lieutenant Collingsworth should handle him. Curtin and Kelly followed O'Connell into the building over the shouts and threats of Parelli, who had his arms being held behind him by one of the bigger MP's, while Collingsworth took his gun away from him.

For such a small building it could have really packed a punch, inside there were enough armaments to blow a hole in the city. There were crates stacked to the high ceiling with narrow pathways just big enough to squeeze through. Curtin, and especially Kelly, didn't know what half of it was.

O'Connell had acquired a clipboard somewhere and was making notes while they walked through the maze. At one point he stopped, looking back at Curtin indicating an open crate on the floor. The side of the crate had a bunch of lettering and numbers, but the important words were Military Armament Company (MAC-10).

"There were ten in this crate, Tom," O'Connell said. "You had one, we found one in Parelli's car, that I assume he got from the *escapee*? There are two left in the crate, so there are six more out there."

Curtin nodded acknowledging, but was looking at another open crate. He grabbed Kelly by the arm. "Come on Kelly, we need to get going."

Kelly didn't know where they were going, but one word on the box Curtin was looking at got his attention, '*Incendiary*'.

Just then Lieutenant Collingsworth came around the

corner and stopped Curtin and Kelly's retreat mainly, because the lane was so narrow.

"Captain, what do you want us to do with the civilians?" MP's didn't give a shit who anyone was. Cops? Generals? It didn't matter to them.

O'Connell looked at Curtin for an answer. Curtin said. "Hold them for a minute or two will you Lieutenant?" Then to O'Connell he said, "Thanks for this, Ray. I owe you one."

"Another one, you mean." O'Connell smiled. He was going to look like a genius with this confiscation of weapons.

"Oh, and Ray, can you have someone give Parelli and the boys a medal or something. Nothing flashy." Curtin added smiling.

"Will do." O'Connell's mind was already somewhere else as he turned and jotted down the numbers from another crate he was looking at.

When Curtin and Kelly emerged from the building, Parelli and his men were milling around the little parking lot, not being detained, exactly, but not allowed to leave. The MP's were searching their squad cars, making sure that none of the things inside the building had sneaked out and hidden themselves in the trunks of the cop cars.

Ignoring Curtin when he walked past, Parelli was acting like he was still in charge. He had already lost it once and was determined to continue to pose as a superior officer. He would deal with Curtin later.

He was going to ignore Curtin, that is, until Curtin got

into Parelli's personal squad car with Kelly in the passenger seat and drove out of the lot, spinning the tires until they smoked. Parelli had to be restrained again. At least it was by his own men this time and not as demeaning as having a big MP hold his arms behind his back. It wasn't exactly superior officer behavior though.

Chapter 78: The Assault Team

They were in two cars, heading south. A Buick and a Ford LTD. Father Regan had stolen them. His survival training on the streets of Belfast as a child always came in handy. The license plates had also been switched with ones that had been stolen from the long term parking lot at the airport. No one had any form of identification on them. They didn't want to take a chance of being traced back to the Boys Home.

Halloran and the Frenchmen, Louis and Peres were in the Buick. Peres was driving. In the Ford, were Hans, Kroner and Father Shaun Regan who was of course the driver. They had discovered the whereabouts of the children by following the nurse who had worked at the Audy Home. She had been tailed by Orlando to a large house on the far south side of Chicago.

Father Orlando had also observed a man fitting the description of the policeman Kelly going to the house. He and Curtin would be a different story, they would not go quickly. They had to disclose the whereabouts of the money they had stolen and wringing that information out of them would be a pleasure.

It was a simple plan, Peres and Louis would go in through the front, while Hans and Kroner watched the rear and waited for the signal that the house was secure. Halloran would coordinate from the front yard, Regan would be the street guard, watching for any interference from police or neighbors. This was a total elimination mission. Any police or nosey neighbors would not survive to be witnesses against the Mendalin's.

Chapter 79: The Washington's

Curtin was driving like a mad man, but that wasn't unusual. That was how he always drove. What was bothering Kelly was that Curtin had asked him if he had a gun? Curtin never carried a gun unless he intended to use it and the absence of incendiary grenades from the warehouse had apparently given him cause to need a weapon.

"My eyes on the Boys Home told me that the priests were back in the building although there were no boys present. There were some new faces, however I didn't think they were going commando." He shouted to Kelly, while fishtailing around a corner at 47th and Cottage Grove heading for Lake Shore Drive.

Curtin was angry with himself for being complacent. He never thought the priests would kill the children now. What was the point? The incendiary grenades told him that they intended to do a lot more than that.

Kelly was trying to find something to hold onto to keep from bouncing all over the front seat. "All I have is my snub nose." He said. Five shots weren't a match for a weapon that fired 1250 rounds per minute. Much less six weapons that fired 1250 rounds per minute.

Within a few minutes, they were in front of the Washington's home. The little church bus was in the

circular driveway, everything was quiet. Kelly breathed a sigh of relief. Kay's little Dodge Dart was also in the drive.

After they got out of the car, they checked the yard and surrounding area, finding nothing. When they rang the doorbell, before the chimes even started the door was immediately opened by the Dali Lama or maybe it was Buddha. It was a tossup.

It was Mr. Washington dressed in silk robes, saffron and gold, that covered everything but his perfectly round head. Cecil had noted their arrival. Nothing avoided his scrutiny. He had watched them check around the house, realizing that this wasn't a social call.

When they were ushered into the foyer, Kelly saw that the boys were also dressed in the same kind of monk robes, Nguyen too. They all smiled at Curtin and Kelly, bowing in unison.

"Nguyen told me that these boys are Buddhists and from what I can tell he teaches the same lessons as Jesus so we's going to go down to the basement and meditate over some of Gods teachings with Nguyen doing the driving, so to speak." Mr. Washington was dead serious, but Kay and Mrs. Washington were behind him smiling. Kelly tried to keep a straight face not wanting to get on the bad side of Mr. Washington.

Before Curtin could alert them of the danger the door burst open and two men armed with wicked looking weapons ran in and ordered everyone to remain still. The suppressors attached to the barrels of the MAC 10's only made them look more menacing. Everyone was frozen in place, the order not to move wasn't necessary.

One of them whistled and Father Halloran came through the door followed by two more men all dressed in black fatigues wearing combat boots, they were also carrying the same machine guns. All except Halloran, who had his hands on his hips and a big smile on his face.

"Well, isn't this nice, everybody that I want, all in one place." He was beaming. "And Curtin and Kelly too. There are some big surprises in store for…………."

One of the priests, Peres, had moved over to the end of the row of boys and nudged Nguyen with the barrel of his weapon. A weird thought came to Kelly when he saw that. He and Curtin had been trained by the same Range Master, a sergeant they all called Tex.

Tex was a redneck who had grown up in a circus and could shoot the dots off a playing card at a hundred feet with a revolver. He taught the recruits that the most important thing to remember was that a gun was for shooting people, not for threatening someone or poking people to get them moving.

Tex always said, "*Bullets go far, you don't have to be right on top of someone to shoot them. Get too close, the guy's libel to take that gun away from you and stick it up your ass!*"

And that's sort of what happened. Nguyen grabbed the barrel of the weapon and pulled. Not wanting to let go, the priest was pulled forward, the gun discharged several rounds into the floor where Nguyen had directed the barrel.

Nguyen stepped into the priest striking him in the throat, fingers extended. The crunch of the priest's trachea was audible. Unable to breathe, Peres dropped his weapon, grabbing his ruined throat, his eyes went wide without oxygen going to his brain.

A split second later more shots rang out, the boys all fell to the floor. Being raised in a war zone had taught them that, but Mrs. Washington, Kay and the rest just stood there in the line of fire. Except that none of the priests were firing.

The shots were coming from under the robes of Cecil Washington. The expansion of the gas from the cartridges firing was billowing his robes but the bullets flew straight and true.

The priests had turned their weapons towards Nguyen and the dying priest, momentarily forgetting about the rest of the people they were supposed to be covering. They never got a shot off before they were each shot numerous times by what could only be the silver six-shooters that Mr. Washington wore each day while he protected the public.

Today, they were doing it again. He shot Louis and Hans, who were on the edges of his field of vision simultaneously, center torso, left hand or right hand it didn't matter, he was ambidextrous and deadly with each.

Then, he shot Kroner with both guns in the chest, bullets striking him one inch apart. Moving back to the first two, who hadn't even realized they had been shot yet, he put a couple more slugs into each of them. The three dead priests sank to the floor in unison.

Halloran had showed no weapon so Washington was saving

him for last. To be on the safe side though, he put two rounds into the choking priest in case he had any ideas of picking up the weapon lying in front of him. When he swung back to Halloran all he saw was the man's back as he ran out of the house.

It all happened so fast. When Kelly finally managed to fumble his snub nose revolver out of his holster, there was no one to shoot. Curtin grabbed the gun out of his hand.

"Stay here and call my brother." Curtin said and bolted out the door, before Kelly could ask him which brother.

"That's parquet!" Mr. Washington said. Kelly looked at him like he was crazy, not a big stretch.

"Parquet Boy. That floor is parquet. Get them bodies off my floor. I don't want no blood on my parquet. Take them out in the yard. It's good for the grass." Kelly was dumbstruck. Then they heard three shots, followed by two more. Sounded like Curtin was out of bullets.

Kelly ran to the door, but all he saw were the tail lights of two vehicles speeding away. There was nothing to do but to attend to the task that Mr. Washington had given him.

"Okay boys, we's gonna have to do some tall mediating over this. Don't you think, Mr. Nguyen?" *Mister* Nguyen? The man with hidden talents, had just been given a promotion.

"Come boys, let's go down and have us a prayer for these misguided souls." He started herding the boys toward the basement stairway.

Kay had started to examine the bodies for possible life signs and Kelly went to kneel next to her in an attempt to help her, but she shook her head. He felt helpless.

Before he followed the boys down the stairs, Mr. Washington read Kelly's mind. "Don't you worry about that Curtin boy, he can take care of his self. Just make that call he wanted, and get dem damn bodies off my parquet floor. I can't be shootin these Cat'lics for you all the time. You Cat'lics got to take care of your own problems." With that he turned in a swirl of saffron and gold silk, that was powder burned and shot full of holes, and disappeared.

Chapter 80: The Chase

By the time Curtin reached the front porch, Halloran was already across the lawn and almost to the street where two vehicles were parked at the curb. He didn't shoot, Halloran was too far away and he didn't want to waste ammunition.

When Halloran reached the vehicles Curtin realized he was shouting to someone who was inside the vehicle in the rear. Then he saw the barrel of a MAC 10 come out of the window. So much for saving bullets. Curtin let three rounds go in the direction of the open window and the MAC 10 slipped from the shooters hands, falling into the street.

Halloran saw it too, changing directions he jumped into the first vehicle and took off. Curtin shot his last two rounds in a feeble attempt to stop the fleeing car, then ran to the remaining vehicle.

The driver was hit in the forehead, the bullet hadn't enough power left to exit the back of the man's head, but it had done its job. Curtin pushed the dead man over into the passenger seat, jumped in behind the wheel and sped off after the retreating tail lights of Halloran's get-a-way car.

Halloran headed north. Curtin hoped he was going to the Boy's Home. If Kelly had already made that call maybe backup could reach there in time to help. Halloran turned east and jumped onto Lake Shore Drive, at 79th Street. By the time Curtin turned onto the Drive, Halloran was doing a hundred and pulling away. Curtin floored it.

Curtin was punishing the Ford, it was catching up to the

Buick Halloran was driving. They both had the needle on their speedometers buried in the red zone. When they went around the curve at the Museum of Science and Industry, Halloran almost lost it, but recovered. The Ford handled the curve better, but Curtin let off the pedal a bit. There was no use getting killed crashing at a hundred miles an hour, Halloran wasn't going anywhere where Curtin couldn't find him.

When they were approaching 39th Street, Curtin expected Halloran to take the exit and head toward the Boy's Home. Halloran didn't even slow down. When he did slow down, Curtin quickly figured out what he was up to.

Halloran ran off the side of the Drive up onto the grass parkway and slid the car to a stop just short of the pedestrian walkway that went over the tracks and the Drive and ended right at the door to Father Brown's Home for Boys.

Curtin followed and purposely crashed his vehicle into the Buick in an attempt to crush the priest but Halloran managed to get out of the way and started up the stairs of the overpass. Curtin ran after him and caught him by the ankle at the top of the staircase, twisting it as hard as he could. Halloran had a pistol in his hand, which he dropped. When it skidded off the stairs, he kicked Curtin in the head with his other foot, Curtin almost blacked out.

Halloran got up limping and started across the bridge. Curtin had to wait a second for his head to clear but started after him as best as he could. When they were nearly halfway across, Halloran stopped turned and charged Curtin, who wasn't expecting the move.

At the very last moment, Curtin managed to fumble Kelly's empty gun out of his pocket and he wacked Halloran across the head with it, opening a huge gash in the priest's forehead. Halloran grabbed Curtin in a bear hug and attempted to throw him off the bridge.

Curtin dropped the snub nose. His arms were pinned. The only thing he could see was Halloran's ear, which he locked his jaws onto. Halloran screamed and let go of Curtin, who was suspended in midair over the edge of the bridge for a second, holding on only with his teeth.

Halloran swatted at Curtin like he was a giant horse fly biting his ear off and Curtin let go when he managed to get a hold of the bottom bar of the railing that ran along the sides of the bridge. Halloran took off towards the other end of the span holding his ruined ear, with blood running into his eyes from the gash on his forehead.

Curtin could feel the wind rush by every time a vehicle passed under him at fifty miles an hour. He took a deep breath and heaved himself up, just getting his leg onto the edge of the bridge. When he got his whole body onto the span, he laid there taking a second to catch his breath. The first thought that came to him was that they needed to put a safety fence up along this thing. The second thought was Halloran. He forced himself to his feet and took off after him.

Halloran was already on the other side when Curtin caught up with him. Curtin was still groggy from being kicked in the head. He was lucky he had injured Halloran's ankle bad enough to slow him down. Halloran turned and dropped into a fighting stance, wiping the blood from his left eye as best he could. Curtin socked him in it for good measure.

They went at each other like mad dogs. Halloran karate style, Curtin, south side street fighter style. Halloran landed a round house kick that caught Curtin in the ribs, he heard and felt the rib crack, he could only hope it didn't splinter and puncture his lung.

After that Curtin kept out of the big man's way while he worked over that bloody eye, also getting in as many solar plexus shots as he dared until Halloran started to buckle. Then Curtin went in with the knock-out flurry they taught him in Golden Gloves.

That finished Halloran, when he went down Curtin jumped on his chest, grabbing two handfuls of his hair, intending to bash his head into the pavement until it was mush. That's when Orlando appeared out of nowhere and delivered a hard chop to the back of Curtin's neck, turning his lights out.

Chapter 81: The Home

When Curtin started to come around the first thing he realized was that he couldn't move his arms or legs. He didn't open his eyes, preferring to continue to be considered unconscious while hoping to pick up some information before the show started. He knew that he was going to be the star attraction.

Whack! Curtin didn't scream, but couldn't hide his body's reaction to being whipped with something.

"I see you're awake, Mister Curtin. You can open your eyes now."

When he opened his eyes he found himself staring into the cold gray eyes of Father Antonin Brown. He was holding a long loop of brown beads in his right hand.

Brown started whipping Curtin with the rosary, a maniacal expression of pleasure on his face. When he struck the spot on Curtin's cracked rib, he jerked reflexively. After ten or twelve lashes, Brown stopped. Curtin kept silent.

"Now that I have your attention." There was perspiration beading on his forehead. Curtin looked from Brown to the other two occupants of the room. Halloran was there with a bandana around his head, either red, or white, soaked with blood, he managed a grin at Curtin's predicament no doubt looking forward to the coming activities which would end badly for Curtin. Curtin also noticed Halloran had several teeth missing, but didn't think gloating over it would improve his situation.

The other man was wearing a robe like Brown. He was small and Asian or Spanish. He wasn't smiling and didn't look like he ever smiled. Curtin could quickly size up an opponent and determined that this man was the most dangerous person is the room. He looked around the room and realized he was in the office of the Boy's Home. He looked down and saw that he had been wired to a chair. There was no wiggling out of these bonds.

"You may recognize that chair, Mister Curtin. It's the one you tortured and murdered Father Francis in."

"I've got a picture I can send you," Curtin wanted Brown to lose control.

Brown went into a frenzy giving Curtin another dozen or so lashes before he calmed himself. He was sweating profusely now, wiping his brow with the sleeve of his robe. Curtin kept silent.

As if reading Curtin's mind, he said, "Let's not be in a hurry though. Before we're through you're going to tell us where the money is and a few other things that I wish to know. First, I think I will let Father Orlando do a little whittling on you to get your tongue loosened up."

The little priest produced a wicked looking knife out of his sleeve that glinted in the candle light coming from several wall sconces that were the only illumination in the room. He didn't grin, but Curtin could see he was anxious to get started.

Curtin looked around for a possible reprieve, but there seemed to be no escape from this predicament. He heard a horn outside, just a quick beep, a police siren would have been better.

Brown noticed, too. "Don't think about rescue. These walls are two feet thick and the doors have pick proof locks. This is the end for you and your....whatever it was that caused you to meddle in my affairs."

"Listen, we can make a deal. I'll give back all the money. Just let me go and....." Brown started whipping him again and Curtin screamed like he was on fire.

"Please!" He begged.

"Don't whip me anymore," he screamed at the top of his lungs. "I'll tell you whatever you want to know, just keep that guy with the knife away from me."

"Oh you're going to do all those things regardless and when Orlando gets through with you you're going to be planted down in the basement next to Father Francis. That's the kind of justice you deserve."

"Well, if you're going to kill me, will you please hear my confession first?" Curtin was crying like a baby with colic.

"Confession?" Brown said incredulously. "You want absolution from me?" Brown was smiling now. He looked over at Halloran who shook his head at the absurdity of the idea.

"Please, Father. I don't want to die with all of these sins on my soul," Curtin was pleading with him.

"What sins do you want to confess?" Brown was curious.

"Well, I stole all that money and I burned up those two guys in that car," Brown frowned at the thought.

"Then there was Father Francis, it was a pleasure to kill that freak, and the army guy and the other two priests at the warehouse I burned down." Brown was starting to boil at the recounting of all of the mayhem this man had caused.

Curtin went on. "Oh, and Father Adolphus at the Seminary. I wish I could have given the Abbott the Torquemada treatment too, but I didn't get the chance."

Brown looked over at Orlando, ready to unleash him on this man who bragged about killing priests.

"Then there was what.....five more tonight?" Brown was through listening to this, he signaled to Orlando and stepped back.

"And of course the three of you." Curtin said.

"The three of us?" Brown raised a finger and stayed Orlando with the gesture. "You want to confess to killing us? Just how do you think you are going to accomplish that?"

Just as he started to laugh there was the *Pfffft* of a silenced weapon and Father Orlando's left eye disappeared, a plume of material exploded from the back of his head. Halloran started to turn and the next *Pfffft*, a second later, hit him in the eye tearing off the bandanna he had wrapped around his head when it exited. Both priests sank to the floor. Brown was frozen in place with only his rosary in his hand.

"That's my brother you're whipping." Curtin couldn't turn to

see who it was, but the voice was clear and welcome. It was
Michael.

Chapter 82: Judgment

Before he became a priest, Michael Curtin was the top agent in the OSS. He traveled all over the world performing feats of espionage and assassination for the Western Powers. He was recruited by the Vatican and was sponsored to the priesthood by Pope Paul VI himself, ordained in a private ceremony, in St. Peter's Basilica. The secrecy surrounding Michael was necessary, because he was slated for a special role.

As years went by he took the time to teach his little brother Tommy everything he knew. Curtin had idolized Michael, but had always taken for granted that his oldest brother was special and had special talents. The young Curtin was eager to learn and kept the identity of his teacher a secret, even from his closest friend, Jim Kelly.

"Do you know who I am, Father Brown?" Michael said calmly. Brown just glared at him.

"My name is Michael, and I am a follower of Francis of Assisi the first person to receive the miracle of the *real* Stigmata from our Lord. I am named for the Archangel Michael, Saint Michael, although he existed long before the Church started naming saints. Michael defeated Satan in the war for heaven, and cast him down. Michael leads the Army of God and is the true Angel of Death. *He* is the true guardian of the Church."

"I don't need you to tell me bible stories, just shoot me and get it over with," Brown sneered. The man who had tortured and killed countless humans wasn't expecting any more mercy than he had given his victims.

"We're coming to that. First, however, I offer you a chance to confess your sins to God and ask for forgiveness. More than you were going to do for my brother," he pointed out.

"To you!" Brown spat at Michael.

"Your choice. Maybe you don't believe in heaven or hell." He emphasized the word *hell*. Michael went on before Brown could say anything else. He really wasn't interested, just doing his job.

"The second matter is that of judgment."

"Judgment? Who are you now? God?" Brown said.

"Don't be in such a hurry to see God. I'm talking about the judgment of the Roman Catholic Church. You were given an edict by the Holy See that gave you permission to conduct your...ah...missions around the world." Michael sounded like a judge handing down a court order.

"Well, I'm here to tell you that your edict has been rescinded. You have been defrocked. Your privileges to say mass and basically anything else are officially rescinded. Your crimes against humanity, especially innocent children, have been exposed and will not be tolerated. The Catholic Church has a long history of some of its members behaving badly, but they are merely motes in God's eye. The church also has a long history of holding these people accountable for their sins. You are being judged. Not in a civil court. In these matters, we are above the laws of man."

There was a glimmer of hope in Brown's eye, was there a chance the Vatican would allow him to escape this mess in return for his silence regarding all of the activity that went on concerning the Mendalin's? Of course, the public disclosure of such a radical faction within the Catholic Church would be damaging to the bottom line. He knew things about hundreds of priests, no thousands. Maybe, there was a chance.

"What are you saying?" Brown questioned.

"I told you my name, it's not just a name. I am the true guardian of the Church and the Vatican has basically left it up to me. You don't wish to confess, fine. I offer you the chance to speak." Michael just stood there with his hands to his sides, completely unreadable.

"I have money....." Brown offered.

Michael laughed, "That's how you bargain for your soul? The judgment is death." Before Brown could barely register Michael's words, he raised the Beretta and shot the Mendalin in his left eye. The same as the other two. Only the surprised expression on ex-Father Brown's face was different.

"Will you get me out of this chair?" Curtin screamed at him. Michael walked around behind the chair stepping over Brown who still had the beads in his hand, and started untwisting the wires that secured Curtin.

"Where the hell were you? That son of a bitch was whipping the shit out of me! When I heard the horn beep I cranked up the volume, but then when you didn't show I thought he was going to let that little bastard start carving me up. How long were you standing in the hall watching the party while I was saying the rosary, the hard way?"

"Quit complaining, you baby," Michael smiled where Curtin couldn't see him, very relieved that he had gotten the door lock open in time to save his little brother from being eviscerated by that priest.

"You're lucky I was able to get in here at all. That lock on the front door was almost pick proof, almost. If it had been you, you'd still be standing on the porch scratching your head."

"In your dreams, preacher. Come on, get this shit off me and let's get the hell out of here."

"I hear that!" Michael said, finally getting the wire off of Curtin's wrists. His hands were swollen and blue.

When they got to the front door, the rest of the cavalry was charging up the stairs. Brothers, Pat and Danny, brother-in-law Nicky who seemed to always have two scary Sicilians with him, Kelly and the girlfriend, even Alonzo was there.

"Everything's all right." Michael stopped the charge. "Except we need to get out of here. Let's meet back at the house, shall we?" Everybody turned around, like Michael was conducting a ballet, heading back the way they had come.

Curtin called out to Nicky and they stopped to talk for a second. Kelly couldn't hear what Curtin was saying, but when he was finished Nicky made the sign of the cross two or three times real fast. Then with an unseen command, the two Sicilians followed him into the house and closed the door.

"Where's my gun?" Kelly said.

"I lost it," Curtin said.

"You lost it! That's the third time," Kelly said.

"I'll buy you another one." Curtin said.

"That's what you say every time. I'm still waiting for the first gun I lent you to be replaced." Kelly said. He looked a little closer at Curtin who went around Parelli's car to the passenger side, which he never did, and got in.

"Who beat you up?" Kelly asked when he got in behind the wheel.

"Halloran. That's how I lost your gun. I was pistol whipping him with it and I dropped it off the bridge."

"What a bunch of bullshit! Who's gonna believe that?" He looked over at Curtin's eye, which was swelling shut. "I hope you killed the bastard."

"No, I didn't."

"No? You mean he's still alive?"

"No. Michael shot him in the eye, Brown too."

"Now you're blaming a priest? Your ass is going to burn in hell for sure, Curtin," Kelly smiled. "And I'll probably get sent there with you."

"Maybe not Kelly, maybe not." Then he added, "We have angels watching over us."

Chapter 83: Meadow Lakes Apartments

"This is terrible." Kay Miller thought for the hundredth time. What was terrible was that she was sort of liking Kelly too much. Too much for her own good. She was sure. Nothing good could come from a relationship with a cop. She only hated doctors more than cops, she told herself a thousand times, except Kelly was different. She was developing feelings for him, which was terrible. She had a career to think about. Some career, she didn't even have a real job.

When the door buzzer went off, she jumped a foot. Why couldn't she have nice chimes like the Washington's did? What was she doing? She was procrastinating. She buzzed Kelly in after hearing his voice on the intercom. She had allowed him to come up several times to pick her up for a date, but tonight she was thinking about letting him come up after the date.

The restaurant was on Halsted Street in Greek Town. When they arrived the owner knew Kelly and made a big fuss over them. Kay felt uncomfortable at first, but everyone was so nice that she soon felt *"at home"*, which is what Kelly told her the man had said to her in Greek.

Kelly told her that Curtin was recovering. There would also be no more problems with the priests. She thought they were probably all dead but didn't want to ask. Helping Kelly and Dr. Nguyen drag those bodies out of the house was more knowledge than she wanted to have.

When she had gone back to the Washington's later that night to pick up her car, the bodies were gone and all evidence of the incident was gone too. Cecil acted as though nothing had happened, even the boys weren't upset. She thought about doing a little of that meditation.

After Kelly made his phone call they had jumped into his squad car and headed for the Boy's Home. Happy to hear that the fighting was over, she had triaged Curtin and ordered him to the hospital for stiches, x-rays and a wrap of his broken ribs.

Now, that all seemed far away. They had feasted on flaming cheese, lamb chops and rose` wine from a bottle that had no label. Kelly had drunk more than she and when she said she would have just one more drink he had balanced the glass on top of his head and poured it full without seeing what he was doing, or spilling a drop. She couldn't help, but laugh.

After sipping thick foamy coffee from tiny cups and eating the most delicious desert called Galactoboureko, she was content, she resolved to ask Kelly up to her apartment. First, she had something she wanted to tell him. She wasn't a big believer in fate, but she had seen it at work in the past few weeks.

"Kelly, remember when you first came to the Audy Home with Poc......and I was a little upset."

"A little." He wasn't drunk enough to screw up this date with a dumb response.

"Well, you said something about recognizing my cap and pin. Every nursing school has its own caps and even

Caduceus pins sometimes. Mine are both unique. When you mentioned you were blown up by a field stove I thought I remembered it. I had a friend of mine look up the records and I probably did take care of you when you came in with your injury."

"I knew it!" He was a little drunk. He didn't know shit.

"Maybe," she was skeptical. "If I remember correctly you were pretty out of it from the morphine they shot you up with in the field. But I thought it was an interesting coincidence."

"Coincidence? Captain Miller, I owe you my life. You saved me and now I am at your beckon call for eternity."

"I didn't save you. You weren't dying." She chided him. "But I think I may be driving home."

"There you go, saving me again." He smiled that stupid grin she was beginning to like.

When they got back to her building, they kissed for a while in his little black Camaro, which wasn't very romantic with the bucket seats, so she asked him if he wanted to come up. He jumped out of the car, ran around and snatched her door open so fast she had to conceal a smile. He was acting like a puppy that couldn't sit still for a treat.

They walked up to her building hand in hand and when they reached the steps leading up to the vestibule doors a man literally jumped out of the bushes. Kay let out a little yelp, while Kelly turned to see Sanguini standing behind him with a gun in his hand. Kelly turned to face him.

"I'm supposed to tell you that this is coming from the Cardinal, you Black Irish bastardo, but I want you to know that it's pay back from me too." To emphasize his point Sanguini poked Kelly in the ribs with his gun which was a snub nose like the new one that Kelly had in his holster.

"I think we'll go upstairs and have a little lover's leap party," Sanguini was enjoying this.

Being poked with the gun barrel reminded Kelly of his old gun range instructor Tex again, his admonition of not getting too close to people you were intending to shoot. He also remembered the mechanics of the revolver that he had been taught.

When you started to pull the trigger back it also turned the cylinder, bringing the next round up into the firing position. If the cylinder didn't turn, you couldn't shoot the gun.

Kelly reached out with his left hand and grabbed the top of Sanguini's gun. Sanguini immediately tried to pull the trigger, which he couldn't do because Kelly was holding the cylinder, keeping it from turning.

While Sanguini was trying to figure out why his gun wouldn't shoot, Kelly clocked him a couple of times with a short right hand. Sanguini's head snapped back, but he didn't go down. Instead he let go of the ineffectual revolver and stepped back. Kelly heard a click and saw the stiletto in Sanguini's hand.

Pushing Kay behind him Kelly raised his left arm to ward off the knife. He was still holding Sanguini's gun, but from the barrel end. When the knife sliced into his arm he dropped the gun and started fumbling with his right hand for his own gun, which was still snapped into its holster.

Sanguini continued to slash at Kelly whose only protection was his bare arm. Kelly could feel the blade grate against the bones in his forearm, while blood sprayed. Finally, Kelly got his weapon out and was bringing it up to where it could do some good when Sanguini flipped the knife over with the blade pointing down and plunged it into Kelly's chest burying it to the hilt.

Kay screamed and then there were two loud pops. Sanguini's eyes went wide and he looked down to see two holes in his shirt. That was the last thing he ever saw.

Seeing that it was over, Kelly sank to the ground. Kay was there holding him. Kelly looked to his left and saw the handle of the stiletto sticking straight out from just below his collarbone. He grabbed the knife, intending to pull it out.

"Nooo...!" Kay screamed, grabbing his hand. "Leave it alone, Kelly!"

Kelly laid there looking up at her while she went to work. She reached behind her back and then into the sleeve of her blouse and pulled her bra out of her sleeve. Nice trick, Kelly thought. If he wasn't dying he would have liked to ask her how she did that.

She wrapped the bra around his arm several times using his snub nose to twist the tourniquet until the blood flow began to ebb. Kelly looked up at her.

"If you save me again, you'll have to marry me," Kelly could only whisper.

She cradled his head. "Oh, Kelly," she said.

The last thing he saw was a tear that dropped from her eye and splashed onto his cheek. The last thing he heard were sirens, although in Chicago you couldn't always be sure they were for you.

Epilogue

Well, I didn't die, what kind of a story would that be? Kay saved me, again. Although everything works, my arm looks like Dr. Frankenstein was working on it and I've got a pip of a scar where they carved that spike out of me.

Maybe Kay thought it was fated, she showed me a slip of paper from a fortune cookie that she got on our first date that read, *'Today you will meet your mate.'* Maybe that bull I gave her about having to marry me if she saved me again worked, whatever it was she went for it, for better or worse. One guess which one I got.

Poc and his two brothers are doing great. Nobody knew they were brothers. They had apparently kept it a secret until they found the safety of Cecil and Emily Washington's home. They're going to stay in the big house and be adopted by the Washington's.

Another thing Kay confided to me that I had not known was that Sergeant Gregory Washington, the son of Cecil and Emily, had been killed in Vietnam, receiving the Bronze Star posthumously. I understood now why Mr. Washington felt that God had pushed Poc into his arms.

I guess that adopting Poc and his brothers brought that around in a circle and eased some of their pain. Plus raising three teenagers will keep their minds occupied.

Doing what he did best, Curtin's brother John has arranged for citizenship papers to be generated for every boy. They found families for six more on the north side in the Little

Vietnam area, and Doctor Nguyen is fostering the rest of the boys until families can be found.

All Mendalin facilities worldwide have been taken over by special units of the Vatican's Swiss Guards. Somehow, Michael is taking care of that.

Liz and Nguyen took a list of numbers found in Halloran's wallet and put their considerable talents to work on the Mendalin's Swiss bank accounts.

The boys are technically all millionaires now. The Saigon Soccer Club's role has been expanded and will now support orphans that have been harmed by Mendalin Missionary's around the globe. Although there are bound to be obstacles, things are moving forward. Life is long and their lives have just begun.

A minor crisis developed within the Archdiocese of Chicago in the months after my tangle with Sanguini. Sadly, the New World Catholic Newspaper reported that Cardinal Sloane passed away in his sleep, on his birthday.

The scuttlebutt around the police desk, however, is that they found him face down in a bowl of Lucky Charm's after he had gotten up for a late night snack and popped a heart attack.

"*Magically Delicious!*" That's the punch line that everybody is laughing at when they tell the story around the station. It's like Callahan and the "*Who Shooted You Senor?*" joke, only funnier.

The newspaper also reported that the Cardinal had been struggling with the fact that the Archdiocese was losing priests by the dozens. Early retirements, requests for transfers, and outright resignations from the priesthood caused a lot of commotion.

It is rumored that shocking photos of a dead man with a rosary around his neck were sent to certain priests with a note from one, Tomas `de Torquemada on the back declaring them to be marked for death by the Grand Inquisitor for crimes against humanities most innocent victims.

Many of them took the warning seriously. Which was fortunate for them, but not enough, not enough.

Acknowledgements: Rosemary Mazzola

Barbara Galvin

Other Books by William J. O'Shea:

The Foot Post: ISBN 0-7596-3842-X

The Advocate: ISBN 1-4259-2875-7